MORNA'S LEGACY SERIES

IN DUE TIME

A NOVELLA

BETHANY CLAIRE

Editor: Dee Pace
Cover Designed by Damonza

Available In eBook & Paperback

eBook ISBN: 978-0-9960037-4-2
Paperback ISBN: 978-0-9960037-5-9

http://www.bethanyclaire.com

Chapter 1

I'm not saying I didn't question my sanity the moment I'd relented to Grace's request that I take a trip with Cooper to the present to visit his grandparents, alone, without her.

Still, I told myself repeatedly that I was doing this for Cooper—that he needed it, that it was important for my son to know his grandparents, to see his aunts who were up in arms about our long absence. All of that was true, but what's the saying...from the mouths of babes? It's too true. So many children are too smart for their own good, but my kid really does top them all. The squirt was going on twenty as a toddler and is now six-going-on-forty.

Cooper knew it was more than my willingness to do anything for him, but it wasn't until he told me so outright that I realized just how thoroughly I'd been lying to myself.

We'd just turned onto the mile long, tree-lined driveway leading up to the Mitchell family estate when Cooper leaned forward from his seat in the back and rubbed the side of my arm sympathetically.

"Oh Dad, you must really hate it at the castle."

"What?" His words caught me off-guard. No matter my thoughts on its lack of running water and the questionable hygiene of ninety-eight percent of the population, I'd never complained to anyone about my life in the seventeenth century. Why would I? I had nothing to complain about. I knew how lucky I was to be living such an unbelievably extraordinary life. And I was happy there, but that didn't mean that I wasn't also ready to feel like a normal guy for a day or two.

After arriving in the past, I quickly learned that no amount of time there would turn me into a man like Eoghanan and his clansmen. I couldn't ride a horse all bloody day long without my ass getting sore, and no one was going to convince me to go commando in a kilt while riding. I still couldn't chunk half a tree twenty yards or drink whiskey like it was water and stay standing for very long. Worst of all, I hated kilts–the essential clothing staple among all seventeenth century Scots. They were heavy and cumbersome, and there was something about not having separate leg holes that made me uneasy.

2

Months of living in the past hadn't changed me from being the modern man I was. Despite the fact that men of that time, or at least the ones I knew, seemed to take quite well to women from modern times, the same could not be said for seventeenth century women. They did not take to me very well at all.

"Dad…hello…?"

"What?" I shook my head, returning my thoughts to Cooper. "I don't hate it. I was just ready for a break. I thought it would be a good opportunity to take a hot shower and maybe watch a football game."

"Dad." The tone of his voice made it clear that he didn't believe a word. "You're taking me to Grandfather's. He really doesn't like you."

"He used to." I frowned involuntarily. I really didn't like the old bag either, but I wished that Cooper hadn't been able to pick up on that.

"Yeah, he used to, but then you and Mom ran away from your wedding *and* you quit your job."

"Well, it doesn't really matter what he thinks about me, Coop. You know that he loves you, right?"

I could see my son nodding in the rearview mirror, although his face seemed less sure. "Yeah, he kinda does, but not like Bebop."

My father, Bebop as Cooper knew him, loved people more strongly than anyone I'd ever known in my life. "Grandfather couldn't love anybody the way Bebop does."

3

"Yep. Hey, so Dad, why'd you make me sit in the backseat? Mom's not here."

Once...only once, I'd allowed him to sit in the front seat when Grace wasn't around, and the chewing she'd given me afterward had cured me of any such thoughts of ever letting it happen again.

"It doesn't matter that your mom's not here. It's not safe for you to sit up here yet."

My son was not the sort of boy to pout, not over something as trivial as sitting in the front seat, so when he slumped back in his seat and let out a long sigh, I knew what bothered him.

"Cooper, you know Morna would never ignore you. If she hasn't responded yet, there's a good reason."

Morna, our friendly witch and the one responsible for hurdling us through time, was Cooper's confidant and fellow schemer. Although Morna resided in the present, her magical abilities allowed them to be the strangest pair of cross-century pen pals.

"Yeah, but Dad, it's been four weeks, and she wasn't at her house when we went by. She would have known we were coming. Why wasn't she there? I'm worried about her, Dad."

Cooper didn't need to worry about Morna. By my calculations, the old broad should've been in the ground decades ago, and she was still going strong and no doubt would for some time to come.

"Coop, if I had to guess, she was probably just out tending to the sheep. Don't worry about it. She will respond to you, I'm certain. I have to ask you though—what was in this last letter? I usually help you write them, but this time you went to Bebop. Why?"

Whatever reason he had for keeping me out of the loop made me nervous. It meant he was busy scheming, and he knew he had my father wound so tight around his little fingers he could make him an accomplice in anything.

"Oh that." I could hear Cooper's smile in the tone of his voice. "I guess since I've already sent it and you can't do anything about it, I can tell you now."

"Son…what did you do?"

"Oh, you know, the same thing I've been tryin' to do for months now. I just asked her if she'd found you a lady yet."

Finding me a 'lady' had become Cooper's obsession from the moment Grace married Eoghanan.

"It's not Morna's job to find me a woman, Cooper. I can do that on my own."

Cooper said nothing but made a noise of disagreement. I took his brief silence as opportunity to change the subject.

"So you remember that we can't tell anybody the truth about all of this, right?"

"Of course we can't. They'd think we're totally crazy." Cooper laughed, lifting from his previously slumped state.

5

All Grace's family knew was that her business trip had been extended indefinitely after she'd fallen in love, gotten married, and now, six months later, was pregnant. They also knew that my father and I had joined her and Cooper in Scotland, but that was the extent of their knowledge as to our new life. They would remain oblivious to the fact that we'd all decided to live happily ever after in the seventeenth century.

A sudden loud honk repeated itself as a red convertible came up on our tail, following so closely I reluctantly increased the car's speed.

"It's Aunt Jane!"

Cooper twisted so that he could wave out the back window to her. She waved her arms at us frantically, taking her hands from the wheel. After she nearly veered into the trees, she gripped the wheel once again and Cooper faced the front, slightly embarrassed.

"I didn't mean to make her do that."

I waved a dismissive hand in his direction. "You didn't make her do anything. She's very good at driving horribly on her own."

Next to Grace, Jane was by far the most likeable Mitchell and really the only one who didn't walk on eggshells around Walter. I had immense respect for her. She was crass, funny, and likeable as hell.

"Come on, Dad. Speed this rig up. I want to see Aunt Jane."

I pushed on the gas to keep Jane from ramming the back of us and scrunched my eyebrows in response to my son. "This rig? Where do you get this stuff?"

Cooper laughed, elated that he was about to be free to enjoy his favorite play toy—his Aunt Jane. "I don't know. It just comes to me, Dad."

We rounded the corner that revealed the Mitchell mansion and reluctantly I placed the car in park. Unbuckling, Cooper flung the car door open and ran to the driver's side of Jane's car, waiting for her to open it to him. As she climbed out of the car, he threw his arms around her legs. "Aunt Jane. To the tree," he pointed down the path beside the house, leading to the extravagant tree house. "We gotta go before Grandfather comes out."

Jane laughed but stayed where she stood, shouting at me from beside her car. "Hey Jeffrey, I'd come say hello, but it sounds to me like this kid's got the right idea. I'll catch you later."

Shaking Cooper loose, she took off in the direction of the path. "Race you, Coop. You better hurry." Turning, as she ran, she yelled back in my direction. "Oh! And, I have some big news to share with all of you later."

I called after her as she ran. "That makes me nervous."

"Oh, it should." Her voice faded as she disappeared around the side of the house.

Squealing with laughter, Cooper took off after her, leaving me to unload the car alone. I exited the vehicle slowly, wanting to take as much time as I possibly could. When I faced the house, only one person waited for me in the driveway.

Cooper's grandfather—Walter.

Chapter 2

"Twelve…thirteen…fourteen…what am I supposed to count to again?"

Kathleen Carter leaned her head out of the closet where she worked to busily put away the laundry that should have been finished hours ago, to respond to the voice of her good friend. "Jane? Is that you? Come say hello! I've been antsy all day waiting for you to show up."

She'd not seen Jane since beginning her work at the Mitchell estate. It had been a long six months, but every second had been worth it. She'd tucked away every penny, and now she finally had her share saved and their adventure could begin. Today was her final day as maid.

Kathleen hung the last handful of hangers in the closet and stepped out of the large walk-in to greet her friend by the door. As she approached, Jane turned to smile but held a finger over her lips to quiet Kathleen as the voice of a young boy answered Jane's question, his voice a mere echo down the long hallway.

"A hundred and fifty, Aunt Jane. I need to find the perfect place to hide."

"Okay…"

Kathleen could hear the surprise in Jane's voice.

Jane held up six fingers mouthing silently the words, "*He's six!*" before screaming down the hallway at the boy once again. "I'll keep counting."

"Is that Cooper?" Kathleen had never met the boy, but she felt as if she knew him. Over the past few years, Jane had gushed over him every time she had the chance. She was one proud aunt, and Kathleen knew how excited Jane was for them to make the move to Scotland. She would be so much closer to him then.

"Yes. I'm pretty sure when I was his age, the highest I could count to was thirty."

Kathleen laughed, pulling Jane in for a hug before nudging her head to the still unmade bed. "Here," she threw half of the wadded and now crinkled sheet in Jane's direction. "Now that you're here, you can help me straighten this thing out."

As each pulled a corner, working to get the bedding stretched over the thick bed, Kathleen started to speak and then stopped herself a dozen times, hesitating to ask the question that had been on her mind ever since she'd started her new job.

"Kathleen, get on with it already! You look like some sort of parched fish, opening and shutting your mouth that way."

"Is it terrible that I may weep for joy when this day is over and I'm free of this place?" Kathleen motioned around the room, unable to contain her joy.

She'd known Jane for nine years, meeting for the first time when they were placed in the same dorm room, Freshman year of college. They'd lived together for four years, until their graduation five years ago. As far as Kathleen was concerned, Jane was her sister, her friend, and now, her new business partner.

It was a strange thing to go from racking up student loans in order to get through college to finding out one had inherited a decrepit, ruin of a Scottish castle, worth millions of dollars in historical value alone, but that was exactly where Kathleen had found herself after her grandmother's death one year ago.

Supposedly haunted and near collapse, Kathleen knew it would not only take a fortune that she didn't have, but also someone half mad to attempt its restoration. That was where Jane had stepped in, eager and willing to supply the funds for half the costs of the work, all money from her trust fund she'd never been willing to touch until now.

While Kathleen's inheritance had included some money in addition to the castle, it had not been enough to cover Kathleen's half of the share. As a result, she'd taken on a job with the Mitchells for six months to come up with the difference. Exhausting the job might be, but it had served her well for its purpose. With room and board included, not to mention a

11

generous salary, her contributions now matched that of her friend's.

Pressing her hand over the sheet to smooth out any wrinkles, Kathleen looked up and across the bed at Jane who smiled back at her with understanding in her eyes.

"Of course it's not terrible. I don't blame you one bit."

With the bed nearly made, Kathleen's thoughts drifted to Cooper and just exactly what Jane had been doing before Kathleen asked her to help with the bed making. "I appreciate the help, but you better get back to your game. He'll think you forgot him."

Jane waved her hand in dismissal. "Did you hear how high he wanted me to count? He's probably still looking for a hiding place. But speaking of Cooper, have you seen his father yet? You know, the one I've been telling you about? I think the two of you would get on quite well. He and Cooper live in Scotland now, so it would at least be convenient."

Kathleen knew exactly who Jane spoke of—Jane had been trying to set her up with him for years, but as of yet, Kathleen had never given her permission to do so. "Jane, just because he lives in Scotland doesn't mean it's convenient. I highly doubt he lives right by the castle."

Jane stood, frustrated and finished with their conversation. "You'll create any excuse if it means you don't have to be vulnerable to someone Kathleen, but believe me, one day, when all of your excuses run out, you'll wish very much that you'd taken a risk on somebody."

Perhaps Jane was right, but it was easy for her to give advice that she didn't have to take herself. Regardless, it wouldn't do for her to start an argument with her friend today. Not when they both had so much to celebrate. Instead, Kathleen chose to change the subject entirely.

"Thanks for your help. I'll finish up in here. You go and finish up your little game."

Jane grunted and made her way to the door. "Change the subject all you want—you're going to meet Jeffrey while you're here and, believe me, you'll love him."

Kathleen had no doubt that she would meet Jeffrey if Jane had made up her mind that she would do so, but she didn't have time for any sort of relationship—not with a castle in Scotland waiting for her, a castle very much in need of all the love and attention she had to give.

Chapter 3

As far as Cooper could tell, the only bad thing about the grandness of Grandfather's house was that it sure did seem to be taking a long time for Aunt Jane to come find him. It was fun to find the hiding places, but it wasn't as much fun to actually wait inside them. Usually after this long, he could at least hear her moving around close to him, but the hallway was silent as he hid inside the laundry chute elevator.

His legs were starting to feel all cramped, and he worried about what would happen if one of the maids decided to call the elevator. He didn't want to hear the scolding he would get if they found that he'd actually ridden it to another floor.

Just as Cooper was about to give up and exit his hiding place, he heard his Grandmother's voice calling to him from down the hallway. He waited a moment, making sure that Jane wasn't with her. Perhaps, sneaky Aunt Jane was using

Grandmother to lure him out. He could see her doing that. She was just as ornery as he was. Grandmother continued to call his name. Once he heard her next to him, with no other footsteps, he decided it was safe to peek his head out.

"Grandmother…" he whispered her name softly, so as not to scare her. While she was a whole lot nicer than Grandfather, Cooper also knew her to be pretty jumpy. If he scared her and she screamed, then Aunt Jane would find him for sure. "I'm over here. Aunt Jane and I are playing hide-and-seek."

Grandmother turned to him and smiled, bending over as she whispered back to him, "Are you? Who's winning?"

Cooper scrunched his nose as he thought. He wasn't sure if there really were winners and losers in hide-and-seek since you took turns hiding and seeking, but if Grandmother was asking, he certainly wasn't going to say it was Aunt Jane. "Well, since she hasn't found me yet, I guess I am. What'cha calling me for?"

"Maybe I just wanted to talk to my grandson, hmm?"

Nope. Cooper didn't say that, but he knew that's not why his grandmother called him. She was nice enough, but she didn't really like kids very much. She wasn't like Bebop. She wouldn't come looking for him just to spend time. Instead, he just smiled and waited for her to tell him what was really going on. Eventually, she relented.

"I have something for you. Strangest thing really. I don't know why anyone in Scotland would mail you a letter all the way here when you're just visiting for a week. Why wouldn't they just send it to your new house so that it was waiting for you at home?"

Cooper did his best not to leap out from his hiding place and fall onto the floor in his hurry to snatch the envelope from Grandmother's hands, but he felt his eyes double in size with his excitement. "A letter? I'm so glad, Grandmother. I was getting real worried about her. I think she's even older than you!"

His grandmother frowned, and Cooper realized that maybe that wasn't the nicest thing to say. He didn't understand it really, why old people didn't want to be called old, when all he wanted was for everyone to think he was just a few years older.

"And just what is that supposed to mean? Why would you worry about her just because she's older than I am? And why is someone as ancient as me writing you a letter?"

"Uh…" that was too many questions for him to answer at once. Maybe if he just answered one, she would forget about the others. "She's my pen pal. Mom set it up so that I could learn how to write." Cooper smiled, rather impressed with his explanation—it wasn't even a complete lie, which made it even better.

"Oh. Well, that seems like a good idea actually. Would you like me to help you read it?"

"No!" This time, Cooper did nearly fall out of the tiny square elevator as he stretched his arms as far as they would go to snatch the letter. It would be awful for Grandmother to see whatever Morna had written him. She wouldn't understand, and she'd question everything. "I want to try and read it myself. I won't get any better if you help me."

"Okay, whatever you say." Grandmother smiled as she reached forward and fluffed his hair like he was some sort of dog. Cooper did his best to keep from shrugging away from her. "I guess I better let you get back to hiding before Jane makes her way down the hallway. Just don't break anything."

Cooper shook his head as Grandmother took off down the hallway. What did she think he was…an animal? It's not like he ran around, knocking things off the shelves. He knew better than that. Aunt Jane was much more likely to break something than he was…but maybe that's who Grandmother was worried about.

Once Grandmother was no longer visible, Cooper scrunched his legs up and closed the door to the elevator, enveloped in darkness once more. Truth was, he could make out most of the words himself pretty easily; it was Morna's handwriting he always had trouble with. Usually, he asked his Dad or Bebop for help, but Bebop was at home and he couldn't let Dad read this letter.

As he waited for Aunt Jane to find him, he thought about who else he could ask and then smiled as he heard her approaching. Aunt Jane would be the perfect choice. She would assume that any mention of magic was just his pen pal playing games with him as she always did, and she wouldn't ask questions. She was one of those rare grown-ups that Cooper liked best—the ones that still had an imagination. Grandmother, he thought, could take a lesson or two from her youngest daughter.

Now that he had Morna's letter in hand, hide-and-seek didn't seem like so much fun. He wanted desperately to learn what was inside. Kicking the door open with his feet, Cooper dropped the short distance to the ground just as Aunt Jane turned the corner into the hallway.

"Oh, Coop, I'm sorry! Did you give up on me? I dropped in to check on a friend real fast. I shouldn't have kept you waiting so long."

"Don't worry," he grinned and grabbed one of her hands, pulling her to the staircase so she would sit next to him. "I didn't really wait that long. Grandmother came to give me this," he extended the letter in his aunt's direction. "Will you help me read it?"

"Of course I will. Although, from what I hear, you're a pretty talented reader—quite the wiz kid."

"Nah." Cooper shrugged. It made him uncomfortable to know that everybody thought he was so much smarter than he should be at this age. It wasn't like he tried to be, it was just the way he was made. "I can read but my friend's handwriting is sort of scribbly—I think it's called cursive."

"Ah. I see. Well, I'm sure you'll have that mastered before too long. Let's see what's inside, shall we?"

Cooper snuggled in close, fidgeting with anticipation as Aunt Jane opened the letter. Before she could begin reading,

Cooper reached out a hand to still her. "Oh and just so you know, we have like this make-believe world between us, so anything you read that sounds crazy, it's just us pretending."

"Oh. Okay. Very cool. Thanks for letting me know." Cooper watched as Jane stayed silent for a few moments, reading the letter through to herself before reading it out loud to him. Bebop and Dad always did the same thing. It drove him nuts.

"Come on Aunt Jane, just tell me what it says. I've been waitin' ages for this letter."

"Have you? Well, does your imaginary world with this friend of yours have something to do with your dad finding a girlfriend?"

"Uh, okay, maybe that part's not so imaginary. I was just telling her that I think he needs to find somebody. This lady is real good at pretty much everything. I thought maybe she could help find him a lady." Cooper squirmed uncomfortably. He could see his aunt's confusion but was thankful that she said nothing else as she read the letter aloud to him.

> *Dearest Cooper,*
>
> *I'm sorry it's taken me so long to get back to you. Jerry took quite a tumble you see, and typical stubborn man that he is, wouldn't allow me to use magic to heal him. He required hip surgery, and we have been in Edinburgh while*

he's been recovering. But not to worry, he'll be just fine.

Cooper grinned as Jane paused and looked down at him. "Magic to heal him, huh? You weren't joking about her imagination."

"Yeah, I already told you that."

"Right you did." Clearing her throat, Jane continued.

I know you're worried about your father, but don't you remember what I told you before I left? Everything takes time, and everything happens exactly when it's supposed to. Still, I know it's hard to be patient when we see those around us hurting, especially when they're missing one of the most precious things in all of life—love. Not to say that your father's life isn't filled with love, he loves you as much as I've seen any father love his son, but a man needs more than that, as you well know.

Here's what I will tell you now, Cooper. You're a wise boy, wiser at six than most men ever become.

Jane paused once again to thumb his nose, and she leaned in to him and kissed him on top of his head. "She's too right, Coop. You're one cool kid."

Cooper leaned into her in acknowledgement, anxious for her to continue.

You also pick up on things that most without magic do not. You feel things. Always trust those feelings, Cooper. Even though you're still a kid, those feelings are there to guide you. I believe very soon you will understand just exactly what I mean and, when you do, you'll be quite right I'm certain.

Your father will have his chance at happiness, but neither you nor I can prevent his messing it up if he chooses to. That part is up to him.

I think that's it for now. On your way back home, stop by and say hello. Jerry and I would both love to see you.

All my love, your favorite witch,

Morna

"Favorite witch, huh? Just how many of those do you know, Coop?" Jane laughed as she stood and picked him up. "This lady sounds like quite the character. I think I'd like her very much."

"Oh, you would. I've never known anyone who didn't love Morna." Cooper paused, thinking about what he'd just said. "Not that I know very many people who know her. She doesn't get out too much. Hey, can you put me down, please? I want to go put my letter away. Thanks for reading it to me and for playing hide-and-seek. You're pretty cool, too."

As his aunt sat him down and waved him off, Cooper clung the letter to his chest. He couldn't wait to find out just exactly what Morna was talking about.

Kathleen expected it was in her head, but it sure seemed like Mrs. Mitchell had given her twice the number of tasks to complete today than on any other. She simply couldn't wait to be finished so that she could load up Jane's car and ride back with her to the city, to the apartment where she would pack up her belongings before beginning her life in Scotland.

As she stood in the long hallway, dusting each painting that had been dusted every day for the last six months, she glanced down at her dust rag to see very little dirt coming away off the surfaces. What would it hurt, if just once, she skipped a few and

22

moved on to the next thing on her list? Surely, it would do no harm at all.

Settling to her decision, she slipped the duster away and turned to head in the other direction, stopping as she caught a glimpse of herself in the mirror hanging next to her. Her black bob that fell almost to her shoulders seemed to be getting a bit long, and her green eyes stood out starkly against her pale skin. It was time for both a haircut and some sun, neither of which she was apt to have the time to get in the near future.

Movement in the bottom of the mirror startled Kathleen, making her jump. She screamed as she took in the sight of a young boy grinning widely from behind her. She turned to him, hand on her heart, breathing heavily as she struggled to slow her heartbeat. "Sorry for screaming. You scared me to death."

"You," the boy's arms were crossed but he lifted one finger to point at her, smiling mischievously as he did so, "are so busted."

"Busted?" Taking a breath, Kathleen took in the boy's small stature. His hair was adorably curly, and it hung wildly around his face—a dirty blonde hue that contrasted with his deep green eyes. Kathleen thought him to be the cutest child she'd ever seen. One day, he would be quite the heartbreaker.

Stepping closer to him, she extended a hand, smiling as his little fingers grasped on tightly. "My name is Kathleen, and you are?" She knew who he was well enough but thought it best to let him introduce himself.

23

"I'm Cooper. And yeah, you're definitely busted."

"Busted for what exactly?"

"For skipping all that dusting. And don't you tell me you weren't either because I'm an expert. Trust me, I get in trouble for skipping chores *all* the time."

"Oh. Can it be our secret?"

The boy smiled, making a heart-melting attempt at a wink. "Yeah, sure. I won't tell anybody."

Kathleen and Cooper walked the length of the hallway together, only separating as she moved to the set of stairs leading downward while Cooper moved to the ones going up.

She made it one step down before she noticed that he had turned to watch her. Glancing up, she tilted her head at the look in his eyes. Cooper had both hands on the handrail as he pulled himself up to peek at her.

She waved, wondering if he waited for her to say goodbye. "It was nice to meet you, Cooper. Catch you later?"

"Yeah..." he hesitated. "Hang on one second. I want to look at you for a minute."

Kathleen couldn't help but laugh. What an odd thing for the child to say. "Okay...might I ask you why?"

Cooper smiled, the splattering of freckles across his nose becoming visible as light came through a side window. "I'm just tryin' to picture something." The boy grew quiet for a short moment before he nodded and began speaking once more. "Yep. Yep, I can definitely see it, and I feel it right here, too."

He let his hands go off the rail, and his face dropped so that Kathleen could only see part of it through the spaces in the railing, and she watched him point to his stomach.

"In my gut. I feel it right in my gut. I know just what Morna meant now."

"Who's Morna?" The boy spoke in riddles.

"Oh, you don't know her yet, but you will, I think. Hey, I'm gonna go now, but yeah, I'll catch you later."

With that, Cooper took off up the stairs.

Feeling more confused than she'd felt in a long, long time, Kathleen made her way down the stairwell to the next task of the day.

Chapter 4

The Mitchells didn't realize it, but they lived in the land of awkward. I'd eaten with these people a hundred times, and every time seemed to be more uncomfortable than the last. Grace and Jane's eldest sister, Lilly, along with her husband, Jim, had driven in from the city to see Cooper. With the exception of Grace, the whole dysfunctional crew was present for the late lunch of spaghetti.

The table was so long that, even though we all sat around it, we were separated enough that conversation was difficult. Not that there would have been much conversation even if we'd been placed closer together. The atmosphere was forced, and the ever-present frustrated tension, palpable.

Cooper couldn't stand it and after a while rose suddenly from the table to slide his plate two seats down so that he could sit closer to me. I could see Walter about to reprimand him and quickly threw a look in his direction that stopped anything he was about to say. Walter might be head of his home, but he knew better than to believe I would let him reprimand my son when he did nothing wrong.

"Hey, Dad," he leaned in close to whisper. "What are you thinking?"

"Nothing, son. Well, about the same thing as you, I imagine. Did you enjoy playing with Aunt Jane?"

Cooper squirmed in his seat to move closer, glancing across the table to make sure no one was listening in. "It was great, but I'm pretty sure she forgot about me when we were playing hide-and-seek, but it was okay because Grandmother came along to give me something. Guess who wrote me back?"

"Hmm…." I pulled in my brows, feigning ignorance just to drive him crazy. "I don't know, Coop. Was it Mom?"

He poked me in the ribs hard enough to make me drop my fork before shaking his head forcefully. "No, it wasn't Mom and you know it! Morna wrote me back."

"Who'd you have read it to you? Surely not Grandmother?"

"Aunt Jane."

Jane was really the only sane choice, and Cooper knew it. "Good call, son. May I ask what was in this letter?"

"She told me there might be a lady coming your way real soon, Dad, and she was right! I know who she is. But Dad…it's up to you not to mess it up. That's the part that worries me."

I frowned and turned in my seat so I could look him straight on. As far as I knew, the only single woman within a ten-year

27

age range of myself that Cooper would have seen since we arrived here this morning was Jane, and he was out of his mind if he thought that was ever happening. "Cooper," I lowered my voice. "She's your Mom's sister. I like your Aunt Jane very much, but that is just never going to happen, son."

"What?" He looked disgusted at my suggestion. "What are you talking about, Dad? It's not Aunt Jane. Are you crazy?"

"Apparently so. And just who is this eligible lady that you assume is my perfect match? Are you seeing ghosts around here, Coop?"

"No, but that would be awesome!"

Only my six year old would be excited about the prospect of seeing ghosts. He'd never really been frightened by much, but all of the strange and magical happenings of the last year had made him even less susceptible to normal childhood fears.

"Okay, so she's not a ghost. That's one point in her favor. So who is she then?"

"Her name is Kathleen, and she's a maid here, Dad! I mean shouldn't it be obvious—that a new maid starts working here right before we come to visit?"

Oh, what a dreamer he was and apparently a hopeless romantic as well. If only things really worked that way, to have your love life so predestined. "Well, of course, that's completely obvious. What's she look like? Let me guess—she's about six foot two with purple hair and she's missing her two front teeth."

I did a decent job of delivering my guess with a straight face, and it took everything in me not to laugh as I watched Cooper's face contort with confusion as he tried to decide if I was joking or not.

"Umm....no. Is that what you want your lady friend to look like 'cause if so, Dad, I don't think you're gonna like this girl."

Finally, I allowed myself to smile, shaking my head for emphasis. "Of course not, Coop. Go ahead, describe her to me."

"Oh, she's very pretty, Dad. I stared at her a long time to make sure. She's a little shorter than you, which..." he paused to laugh which I didn't find amusing at all, "means she's pretty short. She has shiny, black hair and green eyes a lot like mine. She has a cool voice too—I bet she's a good singer."

"Hmm..." she certainly didn't sound like a troll. Still, with Cooper's sweet heart, I imagined he had less discerning tastes than myself. I'd never heard him describe anyone as ugly. "She doesn't sound half bad, Coop. There's just one problem...she lives here and we..."

Cooper turned his attention back to his food, seemingly finished with our conversation as he stuffed a meatball into his mouth. He spoke in between bites, his words muffled. "I know, I know...we live in the past, Dad. It's only a small problem really."

"Only a small problem? How do you figure?"

"That's where Morna comes in."

The witch truly meddled too much for her own good, and she really seemed to like using my son as her accomplice. "Cooper, Morna's been known to do a lot of things, but I hardly think she's prone to kidnap the woman and force her back in time."

Cooper shook his head, not bothering to look over at me as he spoke.

"I don't know, Dad. I sure wouldn't put anything past her."

Jane's voice, which neared a shout as she struggled to make sure everyone could hear her, suddenly interrupted any thought I had of responding to Cooper's very accurate comment about Morna.

"Everyone, I have some big news."

I swallowed involuntarily, suddenly nervous. I didn't know why, but before she even spoke I knew whatever Jane was about to say would complicate my already very complicated life. Jane's announcements usually had a way of doing that. They rarely involved only her.

"What is it?" Cooper's voice, ever curious, spoke up by my side.

"Well, as you all know, this is Kathleen's last day here, but I don't know if any of you know why. I didn't want to tell you until everything was in place and we were absolutely sure it would happen, but Kathleen and I are pursuing a new business venture in Scotland. We're moving there next week."

A fork fully wound with noodles, complete with a meatball stuck on its end made its way to my mouth as she uttered the word Scotland. As the word registered in my brain, I missed my mouth completely, sending the saucey mess splashing onto my shirt, smattering a stain all the way down my front.

Whatever I'd expected her to say, it certainly hadn't been that. I'd been right. This definitely complicated things. Jane undoubtedly assumed that her move to Scotland would put her a lot closer to Grace and Cooper. Unfortunately, what she didn't understand was that we would be very far away from her indeed—by nearly four hundred years.

Chapter 5

"Dammit." I stood, staring down at the mess I'd just made, still shocked by Jane's latest news. "That's definitely going to leave a stain."

"No, it won't." Jane stood with me, waving me into the kitchen as the rest of the table looked at me, silently condemning my clumsiness. I had to restrain to keep from flicking a spoonful of sauce on each of them.

As soon as we got into the kitchen, Jane turned to dab at some of the sauce with a napkin. "We'll be able to get it out—or should I say, Kathleen will. Have you met her yet?"

Kathleen again. Even if Cooper was right, even if she were the woman of my dreams, Kathleen-whatever-her-last-name, was the last thing I needed to worry about right now. Right now, I needed to figure out what we needed to do about Jane and her sudden move to Scotland. Things were complicated enough without introducing more people to Morna and her time-traveling, meddling ways.

"No." I took the napkin from Jane's hands and started blotting away at the tomato-stained mess. I only succeeded in making it worse. "I haven't yet had that pleasure, but Cooper seems to have taken a liking to her."

Cooper suddenly burst through the kitchen doors, catching the tail end of my sentence. "For you, Dad! I like her for you." He waved back at the kitchen doorway. "I can't believe you guys left me out there with them. I just couldn't stay."

Jane leaned against the counter, looking back at Cooper and me rather amusedly.

"Oh, is that right, Coop? You know, I don't think that's such a bad idea. I was just telling your father myself how much he would like Kathleen." She turned to look at me. "And you would like her, Jeffrey. And you can meet her now, when you go ask her to help you clean up that stain. She's an expert at stuff like that. I lived with her for years, and I can't tell you how many messes of mine she's cleaned up."

I frowned at the two of them. It didn't matter that I'd like to have a 'lady friend,' as Cooper called it, as much as he'd like me to have one. It drove me crazy that everyone seemed so invested in trying to help in the finding of such a person. Regardless, the stain did need cleaning. It was one of my favorite shirts, and I treat my stash of present-day clothes like they are pieces of gold.

I had every intention of taking this one back into the past with me.

"Fine. Where would I find her?"

Jane shrugged. "Your guess is as good as mine. I have no idea."

"Great." Standing, I pointed at Cooper as I left the room. "Finish eating, then start getting ready for bed. Deal?"

He gave me a thumbs up, obviously excited that I would finally be meeting this so-called Kathleen. "Deal."

"And Jane." I reached out to grab her arm before leaving. "I want to talk to you about this Scotland thing. I…I don't think it's a good idea."

"What? I thought you would be thrilled. I know Grace will be."

"We'll just talk about it later. I'm going to go see to this stain."

I had no idea what I would say to her later. I couldn't very well tell Jane the truth. Who was I to tell her she shouldn't move to Scotland? I had no good reason, nothing that would make her change her mind. But we wouldn't be able to dodge Jane forever once she arrived in Scotland. Sooner or later, all of this would come to a boiling point.

It would all have to wait for another day. Walking out of the room with Jane and Cooper's eyes glued to my back, I went in search of the mysterious Kathleen.

I wasn't sure where to look. Knowing full well the size of the estate, I imagined there was a good possibility I would be at this for hours. Instead, as I rounded the corner leading to the hallway lined with various guest bedrooms, I was brought up short by the impact of someone walking directly into me.

Clearly, neither one of us had noticed the other. We ran into each other with so much impact that I stumbled back a few paces, and the woman fell back hard onto her backside. Cooper's description flashed in my mind.

Kathleen.

Chapter 6

athleen looked up from the floor, eyes wide with shock, at her assailant. So this was the man that Jane had raved about. Well, he'd certainly made an impression, knocking her onto the floor with so much force she knew her butt would be bruised. She looked up at him, already knowing what she would see. She'd seen pictures, of course, when Jane had pulled out family albums to demonstrate that not only was he sweet and charming, but also that he was quite good looking.

To her happy surprise, Kathleen found him even more attractive in person. He wasn't movie star attractive, and he wasn't the sort of good looking that makes a girl's knees weak and her eggs quiver, but he was just the sort of good looking that Kathleen liked the best. He looked real, and honest, and good. He was short for a guy, but taller than her for her nose had been just about equal with his mouth when they collided. He was solid and strong with a handsome jawline covered with just the right amount of stubble.

The one thing that seemed missing from his face was a smile, and the look of pure agony plastered across his features caused Kathleen to bubble over with laughter. Could he really be so concerned about knocking her over? It had only been a short fall, and it was her fault just as much as his. She'd been rushing around the entire day in her effort to finish her last day of work.

"Hey." He seemed lost in his thoughts, and Kathleen waved to him from the ground to pull him out of them. "Mr. Gloomy, can I have a hand?"

Kathleen raised her right hand. He took it quickly, pulling her easily to her feet as he spoke to her for the first time.

"I'm sorry. I should have been paying more attention. You must be Kathleen."

"Yes." He still held onto her hand, and Kathleen used the opportunity to shake his as way of introduction. "And you're Jeffrey."

"Yes."

Still, he didn't return Kathleen's smile, and disappointment started to rise within her. Surely, the personality she saw now wasn't what Jane had raved about so much. If it was, her friend must not think as much about her as Kathleen thought, to assume that she would be into someone so dull and non-reactive.

An awkward silence followed until Kathleen noticed the spaghetti mess on the man's shirt. Technically, she'd just finished her last assigned duty and had been happily on her way to pack her belongings. Now, the sight of anything that would provide an excuse to end this strange interaction thrilled her.

She pointed to the stain. "Your shirt is a mess. Would you like some help with that?"

Jeffrey fidgeted back and forth, and Kathleen relaxed at the gesture. Perhaps, he was just nervous—she remembered his son moving in much the same way. Maybe he was just shy. She hoped so. Shyness could be overcome, but if he really was just as boring as he seemed to be now, well, that wasn't so easily changed.

"Yes. Yes, if you don't mind, I really would. I was looking for you, actually."

He attempted a smile and Kathleen took heart, turning to wave him downstairs and into the laundry room.

"Here, come with me and we'll get you cleaned up."

What was the matter with me? Had it really been so long since I'd been in the presence of a beautiful woman that I'd lost my ability to form a cohesive sentence? I had to have been freaking her out, with the expressionless look on my face and my serious lack of manners or conversational skills.

I was just in shock. While I knew their intentions to be good, I truly didn't expect Kathleen to be the beauty Jane and Cooper had made her out to be. She was. On top of that, she'd been kind and helpful, even though I was rewarding her friendliness by behaving weird and spacey. I needed to get a grip and start acting like myself.

"So, this is your last day, huh? You must be excited."

I could only see the side of her face as she leaned over the sink to start the water running, but the corner of her mouth pulled up in a smile as she spoke. "Oh, you *can* speak like a human. I was beginning to wonder."

Gosh, that was even worse. Not only was she beautiful and kind, she was witty and said just what she thought. I liked that in a woman—a bit of spunk and fire.

I laughed, feeling more confident as I took a step toward her. "Oh yes, I'll talk your ear off if you give me a chance."

She turned toward me, flicking her fingers over the sink to shake off excess water before pointing at my shirt and gesturing for me to unbutton it as she answered my earlier question. "Yes, it is. Then, we're headed to Scotland." A look of panic crossed her face for a brief second. "Jane did already tell you guys right? I didn't just spill the beans?"

I nodded and started in on my buttons. "Yes, she told us. I'm afraid Jane is going to find herself very disappointed."

"Oh God, you're bleeding. Stop right now."

The pitch of her voice caused me to jump as she walked over to me, grabbing my right wrist and holding up my index finger. Sure enough, there was a deep open line in the tip that had fresh blood oozing out rather rapidly. In my shock over Jane's announcement, I'd not noticed it at all.

"I must have sliced it open the same time I threw this food all over myself."

"Here, stay right there and don't touch that shirt again." She ran from the room, returning quickly with a bandage as she grabbed my finger and dragged me over to the sink. I could very well have cleaned and bound my own cut, but I liked the way her hands felt against mine and decided to allow myself to enjoy the moment.

Once I was wrapped up and no longer bleeding, she turned her attention back to my shirt, causing the breath to lodge in my chest as she reached up to touch the button just below my collar. I knew she only worked the buttons because she needed to clean my shirt, but it seemed an intimate thing to have her undress me, and it made every thought in my head fuzzy as her fingertips bumped against my undershirt.

"I'm sure I could manage that if you need to prep the cleaning solution or something."

Or anything, really. I just desperately needed her to take her hands away from my chest. She had to see what it was doing to my breathing no matter how much I tried to hide it.

Apparently, even if she did take notice, it didn't bother her, for she shook her head and kept working away, pausing mid-way down as she looked up at me confused.

"No, you can't do it yourself because I don't want you to risk getting any more blood on the shirt. The spaghetti sauce is going to be hard enough to get out. Why did you say Jane would be disappointed? Disappointed about what?"

I breathed in through my nose, hoping that when I answered her, my voice wouldn't come out shaky. "She thinks that by living in Scotland she will be able to see Cooper and Grace a lot more often."

"Won't she?"

Thankfully, she finished the buttons and stepped away allowing me a moment to compose myself as I shrugged out of the shirt and extended it in her direction. "No. She won't."

"Hmm…" she looked over her shoulder at me as she sprayed a solution over the front of my shirt. "That's a shame." I swore there was flirtation in her eyes.

She was absolutely right—it was a shame. If we weren't around to see Jane, I wouldn't be around to see Kathleen either.

Damn the seventeenth century. Even if Kathleen was intentionally flirting, it would be pointless to reciprocate. In the same country we might be, but unfortunately, not in the same century.

41

Chapter 7

"Aunt Jane...Jane...wake up sleepy head." Cooper crawled up onto the bed next to his aunt who lay snoring with her mouth open, drool dripping out the side of her mouth. He leaned down and blew softly into her ear, knowing it would wake her up.

As expected, her eyelid slowly lifted as she regarded him with a look that he knew had more than a few bad words in it. "Cooooopppppp...what time is it, you crazy kid? Don't you ever sleep?"

Cooper glanced at the digital clock next to his aunt's bed and pulled one corner of his lip down in apology. He knew it was early, he always woke early, but he'd not realized it was still in the fives. "Don't be mad, okay? I usually try to wait until the sixes, but I need your help."

Jane rolled over onto her back, reaching to wipe the drool from her mouth with the back of her hand before slowly pulling herself up to a sitting position. "Cooper, are you telling me that it is five-something in the morning? If you weren't so darn cute, I would pull your head off, kiddo."

Cooper smiled and scooted in to snuggle, knowing it would help brighten Aunt Jane's mood. "Sorry. You know me, I just have trouble sleeping very much. Always have."

"I know. When you were an infant, your mother was so sleep deprived, I thought we were going to have to institutionalize her."

Cooper scrunched his brows together. He was good with words, but that was a big one. "What does that mean?"

Jane shook her head and leaned over to turn on the nightstand lamp. "Never mind. What do you need help with?"

"Dad and Kathleen! I know he liked her, I could tell after he came back from getting his shirt cleaned up, but he's not gonna do anything about it. We gotta make them spend more time together."

Jane sat quietly for a moment, and Cooper knew she was trying to think of an idea. "Well, I'm supposed to bring Kathleen back to my apartment this morning. We've got to start boxing it up for the big move."

Cooper slumped over in the bed. Surely Aunt Jane wasn't going to give up that easy. "So what are you saying? That we can't do anything? We gotta do something, Aunt Jane."

"I know, I know. What if we pretend I'm not feeling well? That I'm too sick to take her into town? Kathleen could drive herself, of course, but it would be nice for her to have some help while packing."

Cooper smiled, he loved Aunt Jane so much. He couldn't wait for her to be in Scotland too, and he didn't care what Dad said, they would see Jane and Kathleen all the time. He knew Morna would see to it that they would. "I think that is such a good idea."

Aunt Jane yawned and sunk back lower into the bed. "Alright. Here's what we'll do. I'm going to go back to sleep for a few hours. You wait until your dad wakes up and then bring him in here. I'll pretend to be sick and ask him to take Kathleen into the city, okay?"

Cooper leaned over to kiss his aunt on the forehead as she scooted down into the sheets to return to her sleeping. He whispered as he slid off the bed. "Okay, Aunt Jane. Sleep sweet. I'll see you in a few hours. Be sure to act real, real sick, otherwise Dad will know you're faking. He spots me every time."

Obviously, she was faking. I could see that the moment I walked into the bedroom. Jane didn't get sick and certainly not with a headache. I'd known Jane my entire life, and I'd never known her to have a headache. My son and his aunt were scheming. Again.

44

"Jane," I lowered my voice in the hopes that Cooper wouldn't hear me as I cursed. "You are full of shit. Wake up and get out of this bed because there is no way that I'm driving Kathleen all the way to the city. I hardly know her. I doubt seriously that she would be comfortable with that."

"Dad!" Of course he'd heard me. "Don't say that word. What's the matter with you?"

I glanced over my shoulder and gave Cooper a look that said, *'I'll deal with you later.'* Understanding its meaning well enough, he stepped back a pace and said nothing.

Jane groaned and reached a hand up to shield her eyes. "No, Jeffrey, I can't do it. My head hurts so much I think I'm going to throw up any minute. You have to go with her. You just have to. She's already waiting in the car and probably has been for some time. She won't mind you taking her, she'll appreciate having the help."

It wasn't that I didn't want to be around Kathleen, exactly the opposite, and that was the problem. I didn't *need* to be around Kathleen. Not when I knew I'd only like her more after spending time with her; it would only leave me more disappointed when we returned home. Still, I couldn't very well leave her sitting out in the car waiting for Jane when she clearly wasn't going.

"You," I threw an angry finger at Jane and then turned it on my son, "and you, are in very big trouble. You both need to learn to stay out of other people's business."

I turned, leaving them. No doubt Jane would bounce out of bed minutes after I pulled out of the driveway.

I couldn't let anything happen between the two of us, not even a friendship. I only had one choice, and I hated it. I would have to be an ass.

Chapter 8

It was only nine in the morning but the warmth of the sun against Kathleen's eyelids as she leaned back in Jane's convertible, waiting for her friend to say her goodbyes, left her feeling quite sleepy. Not only that, but she had been waiting out in the car for close to an hour now. What on earth was she doing? Jane knew how much they still had to get done before they left for Scotland.

Sleep continued to tug at her. Just as Kathleen finally allowed her eyelids to close, the driver's side door opened and slammed shut before the engine roared to life. Kathleen's eyes flew open but Jane was nowhere to be found. Instead, she found herself riding away from the Mitchell estate with Mr. Messy-eater himself...Jeffrey.

Kathleen raised her seatback, turning to look at Jeffrey as he sped away from the house. "Umm...can I ask you what you're doing?"

He didn't bother to look at her while he answered, instead keeping his eyes on the driveway in front of them. "I'm taking you to Jane's. That's where all of your stuff is, right?"

Kathleen nodded, her confusion only growing. Had she fallen asleep and just didn't realize it. "Yes, that's where all of my stuff is, but where's Jane?"

He didn't answer, only pointed back toward the house. Kathleen had to squeeze her hands together to keep from smacking him on the head. What was it with men and their inability to have a conversation? She didn't understand it—how he could possibly get in the car, start it, and take off with her inside, all the while acting as if there was no need whatsoever for him to give her any sort of explanation? She barely knew him after all.

Kathleen reached out and slammed her hand on the dash to get his attention. "Hey buddy, stop the car right this instant or I swear I'm going to unbuckle my seatbelt and throw myself out into the road."

He turned his head and laughed as he spoke, the tight line that had been his mouth cracking into a large, handsome smile. "You'll do no such thing. You're a smart girl, and I don't think you'd risk breaking a leg—not so close to your big Scottish adventure."

"Fine, you're right. Of course I'm not going to throw myself out. Still…stop the car." She said it with as much authority as she could muster and, much to her delight, the car

48

did slow. Once he placed it in park, she unbuckled to face him. "What's the matter with you? Are you always such a pain in the ass? I don't know you. You can't just crawl in the car and take off with me and expect not to at least have to explain what you're doing. Why are you taking me instead of Jane?"

Kathleen watched as his shoulders relaxed from their stiffened posture. He exhaled as he faced her. His eyes were apologetic, but he gave no verbal apology. "Jane's incapable of driving right now, so I was instructed to take you and help you start boxing things up. I'll help you through the day and then head back here tonight so that she has her car this evening."

"Incapable of driving? What exactly does that mean?" He made it sound like Jane was intoxicated, which clearly wasn't the case. She couldn't have even been awake for more than a few hours.

Jeffrey turned from her and placed the car back in drive. "She has a migraine."

Kathleen rolled her eyes and buckled as she faced the front, crossing her arms as she did so. Jane was scheming and, by golly, if this day was any more awkward than the laundry room had been the night before, Kathleen would make sure that Jane paid for it dearly the next time she saw her. "Jane doesn't get headaches."

A long span of silence ensued between them as the Mitchell estate disappeared from sight. Finally, Jeffrey spoke so quietly she barely heard him.

49

"I know."

Unfortunately, my biggest concern had been entirely accurate and as the day went on, I only found Kathleen more attractive. For most of the morning, we worked side-by-side in silence. She placed items in boxes and I taped, labeled, and stacked them as she instructed.

The silence made things tolerable. It was after lunch that things took a turn, and I knew I was in real trouble.

It must have been out of boredom, for I could see no other reason for her to begin talking as she did when I'd given no indication that I was interested in conversation, but talk she did. And talk. And talk. For hours on end. It should have been annoying. It wasn't.

Every tale she told was infectious. She should have been a performer; her ability to deliver a story astonished me. The excitement she showed when talking about her childhood or stories of the trouble she and Jane got in during college was enthralling. Her smile made her skin glow with a warmth that seemed to swim over me, lodging somewhere deep in my gut, making me aware of her every movement, every sway of her hips as she walked.

It wasn't only what she said, or how she said it, but the way her voice sounded as she spoke. Her voice was rare for a woman—deep, a bit raspy, almost masculine. It sounded like an old Hollywood vixen in a black and white film. It was incredibly sexy. If I had to wager, I'd side with Cooper—I bet her singing voice was amazing.

It was stupid and dangerous for me to be here with her. The more she talked, the more I found myself wanting her. I couldn't have her. Even if she'd take me, all that would ever come of it was a one-night fling and, no matter how in need I was of some female companionship, I liked Kathleen too much already to treat her in such a way. She deserved better. Frankly, so did I.

Still, if the evening continued as it was, with each new story, each tiny grin or little bit of laughter becoming more intoxicating than the last, I wouldn't be able to make it through the night without touching her.

I needed to leave here—to bid her goodnight and be on my way back to the Mitchells'.

I tried to find the perfect time to interrupt her so I could take my leave. There was no perfect time.

"Do you usually talk this much?"

For the first time in hours, the room fell silent as she set down the pile of books she'd been about to box and moved to lean against the built-in bookshelf along the back wall.

"No, actually, I don't. Never really."

"Then why are you doing it now?" It came out sounding much more harsh than I meant it, and I wanted to punch myself for being such a jerk.

For a brief second she looked wounded; then, as if realizing she owed me no explanation, I watched as her face grew angry.

"Are you kidding me? You're going to give me a hard time for talking? For trying to be friendly when you've looked nothing more than silently miserable for pretty much every second since I've met you? I was talking because you make me nervous!"

"Nervous? Why?" I couldn't understand it. No one ever found me intimidating.

"Because I don't understand you. For years, I've heard such wonderful things about the man who stepped up to become Cooper's dad—the man who has been a better friend to Grace than most people ever get in their whole life. I've heard nothing but wonderful things about you, always. Then I meet you, and you are nothing but weird and short with me and frankly, right now, you look angry. You do not know me well enough to be angry at me." She paused and threw her hands up in exasperation, her pale cheeks flushed in her agitation. "So yes, I've been speaking up a storm, distracting myself from the miserable weirdness radiating off of you!"

I wouldn't have thought it possible, but I thought her even prettier when angry, making me unable to take a single step toward the door. Instead, I took a step toward her.

"I'm sorry." My chest grew tight as my breathing came quicker, my body betraying what my mind knew I needed to do, which was leave. "I shouldn't have been so unfriendly toward you. It's only that I didn't want to be here with you. I didn't want to bring you here today and help with all of this."

She took a step toward me. For a moment I thought she would slap me. I almost hoped that she would. Instead, her lower lip trembled causing my lower belly to tighten instantly as lust surged through me. When she spoke again, her voice cracked.

"You call that an apology?"

"No." I moved two paces closer, until only inches lay between us. "To hell with it," I could scarcely breathe. My hands shook with how badly I wanted to touch her. I'd reached my limit—I couldn't always be the good guy everyone expected me to be. "No, that wasn't an apology," I gripped both her arms, pulling her against me, "but this is."

I bent to touch my lips to hers.

Chapter 9

One Week Later

"Bye, Coop! Bye, Jeffrey! We'll see you two in Scotland. Have a safe trip!"

As the door to Jane's apartment closed behind Jeffrey and Cooper, Kathleen allowed herself to exhale as she slumped against the bathroom door. Finally, she could get on with enjoying her last evening in the States.

She took a moment to look herself over in the mirror, her eyes lingering on her lips as the memory of Jeffrey's kiss flooded her. It had been so unexpected, such a shock to her senses, that she still didn't know what to make of it, but she'd dreamt of his touch every night since.

The sound of the blender stirred Kathleen from her thoughts, and she shook her head to clear it. She couldn't allow herself to think on the kiss—not tonight. Tonight, all that mattered was a celebratory evening with Jane—a way to mark the end of one chapter and the start of a new one in both of their lives.

Kathleen made her way to the kitchen slowly, stopping in the living room to rummage pointlessly through her suitcase, hoping the gesture would make her sudden absence as soon as the doorbell had rung less noticeable. Jane still knew nothing about what had happened with Jeffrey.

Although Jane had thoroughly interrogated her, Kathleen had relentlessly insisted that her and Jeffrey's day together had been one filled entirely with packing. With mounds of boxes left as evidence of all the work they had done, Jane had been forced to begrudgingly believe her.

Kathleen entered the kitchen to find Jane manning the blender as she extended a drink in Kathleen's direction.

"You drink every drop of that up, because after the second one, I expect you to tell me just exactly what the hell that was." Jane pointed to the hallway bathroom. "Why did you avoid Jeffrey?"

"What?" Kathleen nearly choked on her first gulp, trying to feign ignorance at Jane's question. "I wasn't avoiding anyone. My stomach just seems to be bothering me a bit."

Before Kathleen could protest, Jane snatched Kathleen's margarita from her grasp. "You didn't tell me you were sick. If your stomach's hurting, you probably shouldn't drink this."

Jane knew exactly what she was doing, of that Kathleen was certain. She glared at her friend, knowing everything was about to be out in the open whether Kathleen wished it or not. If Jane was suspicious, she wasn't apt to drop it until she'd received an explanation that satisfied her.

"I feel much better, Jane. Give me the damn margarita." Kathleen reached for the drink, but Jane stood removing it from her reach.

"You're being very defensive, Kathleen."

Kathleen wanted to slap the smirk off Jane's face. "I'm not being defensive. I just don't want to talk about it. Give me the drink, Jane."

Jane raised her eyebrows but moved to give Kathleen her drink. "Do you really think I'm going to let this go just because you don't want to talk about it? You tried to make me think that nothing happened between the two of you, but something did, didn't it? You don't even like tequila and you just jumped up after that margarita like a parched man in the desert. Something is seriously bothering you. Fess up."

She should have just stayed in the living room and plastered on a smile while attempting to act as non-awkward as possible while Jeffrey was here. Then, Jane would have had no reason to be suspicious. Deep down Kathleen had known locking herself in the bathroom would make Jane suspicious. Perhaps, subconsciously she was ready to talk about it with someone. She still struggled to make sense of it on her own.

How could he have kissed her so thoroughly, only to jump away a moment later as if she'd slapped him away? If anything, she'd tried to pull him closer and been rejected almost instantly. The contradiction in his behaviors gave her whiplash, and she remained too embarrassed and rejected to face him as if nothing had happened.

"Fine." Kathleen slumped in her seat at the table, waiting until Jane re-seated herself. "I don't even know how to explain what happened."

Jane leaned forward against the table, resting her head in her palms as she spoke. "Why don't you just start at the beginning?"

"Well, he was weird and rude from the moment he got in the car. And although he did help me all day—moving and labeling packed boxes—he hardly said a word, which made me nervous. And he had the most awful look on his face, like he couldn't have been any more annoyed with everything I said which, of course, only made me talk more."

Jane smiled sympathetically. "You always do that when you're stressed."

Kathleen nodded as she continued. "Anyway, eventually he just came out and asked me if I usually talked so much. There was so much venom in his voice, I nearly cried. Instead, I sort of lost it on him."

"Is that why you avoided him? He hurt your feelings and you were embarrassed you yelled at him?"

Kathleen wished that it was all. If it had only been an argument, she wouldn't be so confused.

"No, that's not why I avoided him. He kissed me. And then he left."

"What?" Jane's bottom flew out of her seat as she danced around the room, triumphantly. "I knew it. I knew he would like you. Why are you avoiding him if he kissed you? That's a good thing."

"No." Kathleen stood, tired and ready for their conversation to reach a end. Jane wasn't helping at all. "It was not a good thing."

Kathleen turned to leave as Jane stopped moving long enough to ask one last question. "Was the kiss not good?"

It had to be impossible for a better kiss to exist, but Kathleen couldn't tell Jane that, not when she knew Jeffrey didn't feel that way.

"It doesn't matter. He had no right to kiss me, not if he was just going to leave without another word or explanation. I hope I'm never in the same room with that man again."

Kathleen stepped from the kitchen, effectively ending their conversation, but she knew Jane didn't believe her lie.

She didn't even believe it herself.

Chapter 10

Morna & Jerry's Roadside Inn—Scotland

“Are you really not going to tell me what happened, Dad?” Cooper pulled on his dad's hand as they waited outside Morna and Jerry's door. For the last week his dad had been out of it; he acted like he didn't hear him at all. “Dad…hello?”

“What? Son, I already told you, nothing happened.”

Cooper sighed, sad and frustrated. He wasn't used to his father lying to him. “I know that's not true, Dad. You've been upset all week.”

“Coop…” Dad leaned over to kiss him on the top of the head. “I appreciate your concern but really, there's nothing for me to tell you. None of it matters.”

How could his dad not see that it was *all* that mattered? Cooper didn't understand it. Why did he not see how much he needed someone to share his life with? Cooper didn't know just exactly what had happened on the day Dad had taken Kathleen into the city, but he could tell that his dad had done something to mess it up. Typical. He would just have to talk to Morna about it, alone.

The sound of footsteps approached and Cooper smiled. He'd missed his old friends and couldn't wait to throw his arms around her and Jerry both.

"Hey Dad, do you think we should have brought Jerry flowers or something?"

"Why would we bring him flowers?"

Cooper shrugged. "I don't know. He just had surgery, right? Aren't you supposed to bring people flowers after they have surgery?"

"It's a nice gesture, but I don't think Jerry would appreciate flowers. Some whiskey perhaps, but probably not flowers."

Cooper grimaced thinking back on the time he'd been sneaking through the great hall after dinner and been daring enough to steal a sip of the ale that E-o and his brother were always drinking. He'd almost thrown up it was so disgusting. Grown-ups had the strangest tastes.

The door handle rattled and Cooper pulled away from his dad, rushing toward the opening door with his excitement, throwing his arms around Morna's legs as soon as she appeared in the doorway.

"Gosh, I've missed you, Morna."

Morna pulled him in close before taking his hand and leading him and his dad inside. "I've missed ye too, lad. I swear ye've grown at least an inch since I saw ye last."

If only—it was Cooper's greatest wish each morning that he would wake up taller than he was the day before. Unfortunately, that hadn't happened in a long while. He'd been checking. "Nope."

"Well," Morna winked at him as she led them to the kitchen. "Ye will. Come along, I'm anxious to talk to ye."

They moved inside the room and Morna turned to face his dad. "Do ye mind going upstairs to check on Jerry? He'll be happy to have some male company, I imagine. Cooper and I will get some lunch started for us all."

Morna was a genius. She must have known how much Dad hated to cook and how much Cooper wanted to speak to Morna alone.

Dad was gone exactly five seconds before Cooper opened his mouth to speak, but Morna interrupted him.

"Before ye say a thing, lad, I need ye to remember that no matter how much we may want something for yer dad, he's a grown man who must make his own choices. I willna force his hand in the matters of love."

Cooper didn't even know what to say to that. What did that even mean? Was Morna giving up on finding love for his dad? "Umm…I don't know what you mean."

61

"I only mean that yer father can be a stubborn, frightened fool, and I canna do a thing to change that."

Cooper grinned as Morna worked at peeling a potato. Cooper might not know what happened between Dad and Kathleen, but Morna sure did. And he'd been right, Dad had messed it up for sure.

"Yeah, he's pretty stubborn. You've been watching stuff, huh? You know who Kathleen is?"

"Of course I do, but yer father doesna appreciate people meddling with his life, and I canna blame him for that. Ye and yer auntie need to stay out of the way and let things happen as they're meant to."

Cooper frowned. This was not the reaction he'd expected from Morna; she meddled in everything. "We were just trying to help."

"They doona need yer help, Cooper."

Cooper didn't like standing next to her while she worked at the counter. He couldn't see her eyes, couldn't tell if she teased him. He jumped to pull himself onto the counter, sitting so that he could look her in the eye.

"Are you telling me that you haven't been helping? How did they even meet otherwise? What about your letter?"

Morna sat the potato down and pulled Cooper from the countertop, taking his hand as she led him to the table where they sat down together.

"I told ye in the letter to trust yer feelings. If ye feel that Kathleen is meant for yer father, trust it, but that doesna mean to meddle in it. I too, think that they would be a good match, but I have played no hand in their story thus far."

Cooper's head was beginning to hurt. He just knew for sure Morna would help him. "But you always…play a hand."

"Some people need me to help them along, some people appreciate it. Yer father is no one of those—surely, ye can see that from his reaction to the situation ye and yer aunt forced him into."

"So, you're not going to help at all? She's right for him I know it, but we'll be in the past and she'll be here and…" Cooper stopped talking. It all just made his heart hurt.

"Cooper," Morna placed her hand gently on the side of his face. "If it's time ye are worried about, doona be. Ye know I can help them with that, but that is all I will be helping with. The rest is up to Kathleen and yer father. That's where the problems will come in to be sure."

Frustrated, Cooper stood and stepped away from the table. "It was good to see you, Morna, but I'm ready to go home now. I think I'll go say hi to Jerry and then get my dad."

Head down, he left the kitchen. If what Morna said was true and everything was up to the foolish grown-ups, all hope was lost. His dad would be alone forever.

Chapter 11

Cagair Castle—One Month Later

"**A**re you sure about this, Jane? Kathleen lugged her suitcase into the back of the small compact, knowing that her objections were pointless. Of course, Jane was ready to see her sister. They'd been in Scotland a month, and Jane had heard nothing from her. If Kathleen had been in Jane's position, she would be doing the exact same thing. It wasn't that Kathleen didn't understand—she only wished that she weren't being dragged into it.

"Then stay. I'm not making you go anywhere, but I'm not going to put up with this a minute longer. I don't care if she's pregnant. I am officially angry with my sister."

"As you should be." Kathleen knew how upset Jane was, even though she did her best to hide her pain by acting angry. More than anything, her feelings were hurt. All Jane had talked about for months was how this move would place her so much closer to her sister and nephew. Then, she'd be able to see them so much more. Jane had assumed that was true, that Grace would want to see her just as much as she wanted to see Grace. The realization that perhaps that wasn't the case had Jane feeling as blue as Kathleen had ever seen her.

Kathleen moved to rub a comforting hand along Jane's shoulders. It was selfish and stupid for Kathleen to try and talk Jane out of this trip, or for her to worry about why she dreaded it so much herself. She would see Jeffrey, of course, but what would it matter? He'd probably forgotten their kiss by now. She had no reason to feel self-conscious around him, no reason to avoid him whatsoever. If anything, it was he that should be ashamed of his behavior. He'd fled from her like a frightened child.

Jane's back relaxed against Kathleen's hand. Taking one last exhale together, they loaded up into the car. Seconds into the drive, Jane resumed her fuming.

"You know what really makes me angry? That I don't even have Grace's new phone number. Every time she has called, the number's been blocked, and I made sure to give Jeffrey my new cell number before he left so that he could give it to Grace. That way she would be able to contact me. How could she have let this much time pass without calling? Especially when she knows I'm here."

Kathleen leaned her head against the window, enjoying the landscape that she knew would remain breathtaking to her even if she lived here fifty years. Unthinkingly, she uttered the first explanation that came to mind. "Maybe Jeffrey never told her. I mean, you hadn't told Grace you were moving here, right?"

Kathleen watched as Jane's grip tightened on the wheel. Obviously, the thought hadn't occurred to her.

"You're right! It has to be that, but for the life of me I don't understand why he would do that. It's not like him. I know you're not his biggest fan, and I don't blame you one bit. He acted really poorly with you, but Jeffrey's just not like that."

"Maybe," Kathleen hated to defend him, but even though it seemed the most plausible explanation for Grace's lack of phone calls or visits, it still made little sense. "Maybe he lost the phone number. There wouldn't be an easy way for him to find it if he had."

Jane shook her head, slowing the car to a stop as they neared a sheep casually crossing the road. "Perhaps, but why wouldn't Grace just come to the castle?"

"Well, she is pregnant. Maybe she's been ill." Kathleen knew there was really no good explanation for any of it. Even with Grace's pregnancy, and even if they had lost Jane's cell phone number, there were always letters or emails.

"Maybe, I don't know. I guess there's no point in worrying until we get there. It's just that something feels very off about the entire situation."

Kathleen agreed. Last evening, as she'd packed her bag for their trip, a strange sense of unease had settled inside her stomach, a sense that seemed to only grow with every mile they drove. Although, she couldn't help but wonder if her apprehension was partially due to the fact that Jane didn't really seem to know where she was going.

"Jane, just where exactly is it that we are headed? What's the address of Grace's place here?" Jane didn't need to say anything. Kathleen knew from the look on Jane's face as she asked the question. "Oh my God, Jane, you have no idea, do you? Just where are we going to go then?"

Jane groaned and tossed an envelope in Kathleen's direction.

"Look at the return address."

Kathleen did as instructed, though it did little to end her confusion. "So what? This isn't where Grace lives. This is the address for somebody named 'Morna.' She didn't even bother to put a last name."

Jane pointed to the envelope that now lay in Kathleen's lap. "That arrived at my parents' house when Cooper and Jeffrey were there, and Cooper had me read the letter to him. Since Grace had never given me the address of her place here, despite my many efforts to ask her for it, I slipped the envelope away when Cooper wasn't looking. He said this lady was his pen pal, so obviously she usually writes to him at their home."

Kathleen nodded, understanding. "So she should have their actual address."

"Yes, exactly." Jane turned a quick smile on her before directing her attention back to the road. "So that is where we are headed."

"One problem though, Jane. This address is at least five hours from us. What if we get there and she sends us right back in the direction we came from? Just because they were pen pals, doesn't mean there's any guarantee they live close to one another."

"Well then, we will just turn right back around and head back in this direction. I really don't see what other choice we have."

Kathleen said nothing as she settled in for what would undoubtedly be a very long day.

The address in question sat in the middle of nowhere and, while it should have taken them only five hours, their navigational skills were not quite what either of them had hoped. They arrived in front of the charming two-story home on the side of the small road well after sunset, and Kathleen found herself very unsure about intruding so far into the evening.

"Don't you think it's too late to knock on their door?"

"No way." Jane jerked her head toward a sign Kathleen had yet to notice. "It's an inn, anyway. We'll just stay here tonight."

IN DUE TIME – A NOVELLA

"Oh." Surely someone whose business depended upon travelers stopping in wouldn't mind being bothered no matter the hour. "How convenient."

Taking a moment to stretch outside the car, Kathleen watched as Jane made her way to the front door to knock.

The door flew open in an instant and Kathleen moved to join Jane as the woman standing in the doorway greeted them.

"Good evening, lassies. What brings ye here?"

Kathleen said nothing, allowing Jane to take the lead.

"Well, actually, I'm looking for my sister, but I suppose we'll also be needing a room for the night if you have one available."

The woman's face dropped into one of sympathy as she shook her head. "I'm afraid we are all booked for the evening. Just who is yer sister? Perhaps, I can at least assist ye with that."

Kathleen frowned as she looked away from the doorway, taking in the surroundings of the inn. Theirs was the only car for miles. She leaned her head in closer to the doorway for a listen—not a single sound drifted outward from inside the house. The woman had to be lying.

"Her name is Grace...Grace," Jane threw an embarrassed look in Kathleen's direction before speaking to the woman once again. "Well, I'm not sure what she goes by now. She's married since I saw her last. Her last name used to be Mitchell."

The woman's eyes grew wide in recognition. Kathleen knew Jane nearly threw her arms around the woman's neck in relief.

"Ah, Grace, aye, I know her. She doesna live all that close to here though. Ye are still a few hours drive away."

Kathleen closed her eyes in a silent groan. Of course they were.

"Do you have their address?

"Aye. Give me just a moment."

With that, the woman slammed the door in their face, and Kathleen turned to whisper to Jane. "She's full of shit. There are plenty of free rooms inside. Why do you think she doesn't want to rent us one?"

Jane shrugged, obviously renewed and excited at knowing she was one step closer to finding her sister. "I don't know and honestly, I don't care, Kathleen. It is the woman's house, after all. Even if it is an inn, I suppose she's free to turn away whomever she wishes. As long as I get an address, I'll sleep in the car for all I care."

Kathleen turned for one more look around at the vast emptiness. It looked like that's exactly what they would be doing.

Chapter 12

McMillan Castle —1647

Enough was enough. One whole month they'd been home, and Dad grew grumpier with each passing day. He didn't care any more that Morna had told him to stay out of it. She wasn't here to see how unhappy his dad was. He knew he tried to hide it, but he sure wasn't doing a very good job, and Cooper hated it.

Sure his dad was lonely, and Cooper knew he was sad about whatever had happened with Kathleen, but that wasn't what made him so un-fun to be around. Cooper knew from watching Grandfather that if you did things that weren't good, it would eat away at you, and you couldn't be happy after doing something you knew was wrong.

Dad had done a very bad thing. Although he kept trying to tell Cooper that it was right, Cooper knew that Dad didn't even believe it himself. And it was something so rotten, Cooper just

71

couldn't keep it inside any longer. It wasn't even fair of Dad to ask it of him.

His dad would be furious that he told, but this was not a good secret to keep. He just couldn't even imagine how mad Mom was going to be when she learned what Dad had done.

Cooper walked through the castle hallways with his head hanging low—he wasn't happy about what he had to do, but he knew it was time. He found Mom sitting in her bedchamber soaking her feet in a big wooden bucket. She'd done that a lot ever since that baby had started growing inside of her. It didn't make a lot of sense to him since the baby was in her stomach, but apparently it made her feet get bigger, too.

He wasn't surprised that she knew something was wrong the moment she saw him. Mom knew him better than anybody.

"Hey, what's that gloomy face for, kiddo? Come here and sit with me a minute. You want to soak, too?"

Cooper moved across the room as Mom reached over to pull another chair seated close to her over by the bucket. Smiling, Cooper stepped out of his shoes and hopped up on the seat to dangle his feet in. All that touched the water was the tip of his toes, but he didn't care. That's not why he'd come to talk to Mom anyway.

"I'm not gloomy. I'm worried."

Mom's face softened and she leaned over to pull him in for a hug, kissing him hard on the top of his head. "Cooper, you worry too much, sweetie. You're going to be gray by the time you're ten if you keep it up."

Cooper refrained from rolling his eyes but pulled away from her hug. Of course he didn't want to worry; he just couldn't help it. "It's Dad's fault."

Mom smiled, leaning back to cross her arms as she looked at him. "Oh yeah? Well, as long as it's not mine."

"No, it's not yours, but this sure is going to make you mad." Cooper hesitated, glancing around the room uncomfortably. "Like maybe madder than you've ever been."

"Oh surely not. Your dad doesn't make me angry very often. He's usually pretty well-behaved."

Cooper nodded. Usually, his dad was. "Yeah, I know. But he messed up, Mom. He didn't tell you something that he should have."

Mom fidgeted and pulled her feet out of the water to dry them, and Cooper knew he was starting to make her nervous. "Okay son, I think you better just spit it out. What did he do?"

Cooper shook his toes over the water and slipped himself off the chair as he paced the room. It wasn't easy to break a promise, even though it was the right thing to do. "Okay. You know how Dad and I saw Aunt Jane when we went to Grandfather's?"

"Yes."

73

Mom now stood in front of him, regarding him cautiously as he paced back and forth, his hand on his forehead. For some reason, it made him less nervous.

"Well, she actually lives in Scotland now. She's fixing up some castle with a friend, and she was so excited because she would be closer to us."

Cooper stopped pacing a moment to glance up at his Mom. She'd grown very white, and Cooper moved to pull her into a seat.

"Do you want me to tell you the rest?"

"Please." Mom's hand moved to her forehead, just like he'd done before. He realized that must have been where he picked it up from.

"Well, Dad didn't think we should tell you because he knew you'd just want to get Morna to send her back or keep us in contact with her somehow, and he thought it wouldn't be good to pull anybody else into all this magic stuff, but I've just been thinking about it, Mom, and I think he's wrong."

Cooper knew he talked too quickly, but now that he was finally telling somebody, he couldn't seem to stop. He continued to ramble as he moved around the room.

"I mean, what's wrong with this magic stuff? I think it's awesome, and why not share awesome things with the people that you love? And I've been thinking about Aunt Jane a lot. I miss her, Mom, and she was just so excited to get to see us more. Don't you think she's wondering why we haven't visited? She's probably very worried. And ya know, if it was me, I think my feelings would be hurt."

Just thinking about Aunt Jane being sad made him want to cry. He had to swallow hard to keep from doing just that.

"Plus, Mom, you're having a baby, and don't you think Aunt Jane would want to see it and know it, just like she does me? I don't know, Mom. I just…I usually think Dad's right about everything, but I don't know. I think this is the first time in my whole life…" Tears were coming now, and he found himself suddenly picked up by his mom as he lay his head on her shoulder to cry.

"Oh, my sweet, sweet Cooper."

Mom held him and stroked his hair as she kissed the top of his head. It made him feel small, but he couldn't deny how much better it made him feel. Sometimes a boy just needed his Mom. He hoped he never got too old to feel like he didn't.

"It's a tough thing, isn't it? Learning for the first time that your parents aren't perfect? I think I was probably a little older than you when I realized it for the first time, but you've always been ahead of the curve."

Was that what really bothered him the most? Cooper hadn't thought about it, but as Mom said it, he thought perhaps she was right. "Well, it doesn't mean I love you guys any less, okay Mom? Even though I know now."

Mom laughed as she squeezed him tight. "Well, I sure hope not. Now," she sat him down on his feet and grabbed his hand, "let's go have a talk with your father. Don't worry, I'm right here with you. Just prepare yourself though—I'm not perfect either, and this baby has shortened my temper extensively. There may be screaming."

Chapter 13

McMillan Castle—Present Day

"Are you sure this is okay? I really feel like it's probably not." Kathleen was really starting to think that this Morna lady had it out for them. Not only had she denied them entry into her home when Kathleen was ninety-eight percent positive there'd been no one staying at the inn, but she'd also advised them to camp for the night on the grounds of an old castle some two and a half hours away from her inn. None of it made sense.

"Yeah, it's fine, Kathleen. Look around. Even if it's not technically all right, I don't think there's anybody around to get us in trouble. Besides, what reason would the lady have for sending us somewhere she knew we shouldn't be?"

Kathleen shrugged as she hauled their sleeping bags and blankets out of the back of the car. At least they'd had the foresight to prepare for the possibility of having to camp. "I don't know, but what reason would she have for telling us she was booked up for the night when clearly she wasn't. And what reason…" Kathleen tossed the bag of stones in Jane's direction, "would she have for giving us these stupid rocks and telling us to toss them into the lake before sleeping?"

Jane laughed and reached to grab her sleeping bag before happily spreading it out on the ground like a happy grade-schooler at summer camp. "I already told you, Kathleen. Haven't you noticed how superstitious people are around here yet? She said this place was supposedly haunted by some crazy banshee and in order to keep her away while we sleep, we need to toss these magic rocks in the water to feed her hungry soul."

Kathleen laughed for the first time all day. All of it sounded entirely ridiculous coming out of Jane's mouth. "Have you been smoking crack? Do you know how ridiculous all of that sounds? I thought banshees were like an Irish thing."

Jane shrugged and walked over to a small bush before unashamedly yanking down her pants to take a pee. Kathleen would never have guessed her old friend to be such a wild outdoorsman.

"I don't know. I don't care either. It was a nice gesture, all the same. She didn't want us to be haunted by the banshee. I for one am appreciative of that. It really would have ruined the good night's sleep I plan to have."

While Jane dried herself, Kathleen turned her head and silently pleaded with her own bladder to remain empty for the rest of the evening. She had no intention of peeing in the woods.

It was a beautiful place to camp, to be sure, with the castle softly lit by the full moon as their backdrop, all of it sitting grandly behind the large pond by which they spread out their camping materials. Pretty it might be, but Kathleen would have bet her last dollar that this was no legal campground.

"There's no way I'm going to be able to sleep out here. For one, I know it's warmer than usual, but it's still Scotland. We will probably freeze out here. And two, I'll be worried the whole night that somebody is going to show up and arrest us."

Jane laughed at her, opening the bag of stones and chucking one so hard in Kathleen's direction she had to reach up and snatch it to keep it from knocking her unconscious.

"Whoops, sorry." Jane walked to stand by the water's edge. "I didn't mean to throw it that hard. Good reflexes. Now, get over here so we can throw our rocks. I know it's probably stupid superstition, but I'm not going to risk it."

"Fine. Then, you lay down on your pallet so you can freeze to death, and I'm going to go sleep in the car." Kathleen walked until she stood next to her friend as Jane motioned with her fingers, until she reached the number three.

Together they tossed the rocks into the pond as the earth shook beneath them. The moon seemed to fall from the sky as the stones dropped into the water, making everything around them go black.

McMillan Castle—1647

For one of the first times in my life, I was truly and utterly ashamed of myself. What had I been thinking to assume it was my right or place to keep such news from Grace? To make the judgment that she didn't need to know that her sister was in Scotland, waiting to hear from her?

I'd convinced myself that I'd done it for Grace's benefit, so that she wouldn't constantly be worried about the complications of either telling her sister the truth or trying to manage keeping up such a ruse while being separated by centuries. The truth was, if Grace knew about Jane's whereabouts, I knew she would be certain that either communication or actual time travel remained open and available at all times, and that took away every excuse I had for being such an ass to Kathleen.

I shouldn't have kissed her in the first place. I'd known that even before I'd done it, but I'd been unable to resist the urge that had surged through me. Then, like a coward, I'd pulled away and fled without explanation, leaving us both breathless and confused and deserving of so much better. My excuse was that

I'd never see her again anyway. Deep down, I knew that wasn't true. I wanted to see her again. I needed to.

And truthfully, in the strange, magical world in which I found myself living, there was no real obstacle that would keep me from doing just that—only the obstacles of fear and what-ifs that lay in my heart.

I lay in bed, in the small cottage just beyond the edge of the McMillan Castle pond that I now called my home, embarrassed and ashamed by the person I'd been over the last month. I hated that it had taken my young son and his spitfire angry mother to wake me up. I owed Grace and Cooper an apology. I owed Kathleen an apology. I even owed Jane an apology for leaving her to worry and fret over her sister's whereabouts for so long.

Tomorrow I would work on making everything right. A travel would have to be made once again and the truth told to Jane about where and when her sister now lived. I wouldn't allow Grace to risk making the travel while pregnant, and no matter how safe Morna swore the magic was, I didn't like the idea of Cooper making such a journey unnecessarily.

At sunrise, I would make the journey alone. Somehow I would need to find the words that would calm Jane's fears and make her believe the impossible.

I had no idea what I could say to her—most likely it didn't matter. By tomorrow's end she would think I was bat-shit crazy and in need of hospitalization.

I lay awake practicing different versions of the speech I would give, all the while doing my best to imagine Jane's reactions. I knew I grew tired but during one such silent run-through, Jane's voice rang so loud in my head, it sounded as if she spoke right outside my front door. I shook my head, to rid myself of the noise. Clearly, it was time to sleep.

I leaned over to blow out my bedside candle when the voices drifted toward me once again. I didn't imagine them. The voices of several hysterical women were coming from the direction of the pond, and one of them sounded very much like Jane.

Chapter 14

K athleen moaned as she held onto both sides of her head, convinced that if she released her grip, her skull would literally split right down the middle. She'd never experienced such a throbbing headache, the onset of which she couldn't begin to understand.

She lay on the ground and slowly forced her eyelids open as she rolled over to search for Jane. She found her friend in much the same position as herself.

"What the hell happened?"

Removing her hands hesitantly, Kathleen took deep breaths as she pushed herself to sit up and then stand. Gradually, the pain receded. "I have no idea, but stand up, it helps."

Kathleen gave Jane her hand, hauling her to her feet as they glanced around, noticing for the first time that the car and all of their belongings were nowhere to be found.

"Oh my God." Jane's voice cracked as she started to cry hysterically. "We were attacked, Kathleen! Attacked and then robbed."

"Jane." Kathleen reached out to grip Jane's shoulder, shaking her to gain her attention. "Stop it. Freaking out isn't going to do us any good. If we were attacked, which I can't see any other explanation, just be glad they didn't kidnap us. Other than a wicked bad headache, I think we both look okay, but we can't do anything else until you calm yourself down."

She stepped away, allowing Jane the chance to take a moment and calm her breathing while she looked around and tried to formulate some sort of plan.

Obviously, they would have to walk, but where? They didn't know their way around very well. At least if they kept their backs to the pond, they could see anyone else approaching them. If they started to walk away, whoever had attacked them before could easily ambush them again. Although terrifying, Kathleen could see little choice but for them to wait by the water until daylight and then re-group.

After a few moments, a much more collected Jane reached out to grab Kathleen by the arm. "Okay, what do we do?"

"We stay here until morning."

"What?" The pitch of Jane's voice was so loud that Kathleen moved to slap her palm against Jane's mouth to silence her.

"Shhh! What's the matter with you? Do you want whoever did whack us over the head to know that we're awake?"

Jane's eyes grew wide with panic. Kathleen removed her hand, knowing she'd shocked her into silence.

"Look." Kathleen backed up and sat down with her back nearly touching the water and waited for Jane to join her. "We don't know our way around here. At least here with our back to the water we can see anything approaching. If we move, we can't. Once it's daylight, people will arrive to open the castle to visitors, and we can get help, okay?"

Jane nodded and remained silent.

Kathleen leaned forward to rub her temples, pushing away the remaining ache that seemed to radiate all the way down to her toes. The sound of Jane's hurried whisper startled Kathleen so much her rear end lifted off the ground as she jumped.

"Kathleen, lift your head and turn around. Do you remember seeing that before?"

Kathleen twisted to see the moon shining down on a small wooden cottage nearly a hundred yards away from them, just barely outlined by the moon's light. She'd not noticed it before, but then again, it could have just been because the moon had been at a different point in the sky.

"No, I didn't."

Jane didn't whisper as she spoke again. "Maybe they can help us." Then she raised her voice to a shout, standing and cupping her hands over her mouth as she did so. "Help! Somebody help us!"

Horrified, Kathleen reached up to yank on Jane's hand, pulling her back to the ground with all the force she could manage, all but tackling her as she struggled to silence her.

"Are you crazy? What if the people who attacked us live in that cottage? They left us alive the first time. Do you want them to come back and finish the job?"

Jane whimpered as Kathleen watched the thought sink in. Together they huddled with their heads turned toward the cottage, both of them gasping in horror as the light of a flame suddenly sparked to life.

"Oh my gosh, Kathleen, I'm so sorry. This is it, isn't it? We're going to die."

Kathleen struggled to stand as Jane gripped her around the waist like a small child, whimpering as the outline of a man started to make its way toward them.

"Just calm down, Jane. We don't know who he is, but if he tries to hurt us, at least we can see him this time. There's only one of him and two of us. So get up off your ass and act like a grown-up."

Kathleen knew she sounded harsh, but she didn't know what else to do. Perhaps acting brave would help her feel that way, rather than the watery sensation that made her knees want to buckle so that she could sink to the ground in her horror.

Instead, she forced herself to address the man as he approached.

"Stop moving right now, mister. We don't need you to come any closer."

"What's the matter with you two? Are you trying to wake up the whole castle?"

All the breath in Kathleen's body left as Jane released her grip and moved to throw her arms around the man that approached them.

Jeffrey.

Chapter 15

"What in the world are you wearing, Jeffrey? You look crazy! And why are you staying in this shack?"

I ignored Jane as I took two paces across the room to light candles, doing my best to illuminate the dark space, but no amount of light was going to squelch Jane's criticism or her utter lack of understanding.

Normally, I slept in nothing, but even in my hurry to see what the screaming was about, I'd had the common sense to throw on a pair of linen breeches and a shirt. Only problem was, to two twenty-first century women, my seventeenth century dress seemed to cause Jane more worry and distress than if I'd stepped outside bare naked.

Her questions hadn't ceased for a moment, and I could tell by the pitch of her voice how frightened she still was. I couldn't tell her the truth, not until she calmed down at least a little.

"I mean, there's not even a bathroom in here, Jeffrey…or electricity! Couldn't you have found something a little better to stay in? I can't imagine that Grace feels very comfortable sending Cooper over here to stay."

I shook my head, tired and frustrated. I had no idea how Kathleen felt about everything; she'd not said a word since I'd approached them, but I could already tell that Jane was not going to be easy to convince that she'd ended up in the past. "Grace has zero problem with my new home. She helped build it."

Jane laughed and, although my back was to her, I could envision her hand dismissing me in disbelief. "Yeah, I'm sure she did."

Kathleen spoke for the first time, clearly just as frustrated with Jane as I. "I don't know why you care that he doesn't have a bathroom. You're the one who didn't hesitate for a second to take a big tinkle in the middle of nowhere."

I swallowed my laughter but smiled into the darkness, still facing away from them.

"Yeah, but that was before, when I was all gung-ho about finally getting my sister's address and hyped up for the adventure that would have been sleeping next to an old empty castle."

"The castle is hardly empty." I'd said it before, even as I'd approached them, but in their panic, neither had heard me.

Jane moved so that she stood in front of me, her eyes showing her confusion. "What? Of course it is."

89

I crossed my arms, letting her question hang in silence as I thought about what I should do. As far as I could tell, only one thing would happen if I tried to convince them they were in the seventeenth century now, in the middle of the night, with no one else to back up my story. Both women, Jane especially, would throw a fit so loud and ridiculous that the entire castle actually would wake up. I didn't see any need for such a spectacle.

The great revelation and the chaos that would follow could wait until morning.

"Look, you two look dead on your feet. You're a lot safer in here than you were out there, so why don't we just all get some sleep. We'll regroup in the morning and find out who was responsible for knocking the two of you unconscious." My teeth ground together involuntarily. It made my head hurt just thinking about how painful the travels are, especially the first time when you don't know what to expect. I felt sorry for both of them.

Jane nodded and yawned, her desire for sleep seemingly overwhelming any other questions she wanted to ask. She moved toward the bed, even before I pointed in its direction. "You two take the bed. I'll sleep on the floor by the fire."

As I moved toward the fire, Kathleen reached for my arm, surprising me by her touch as she looked directly at me for the first time. Much more grounded than Jane, she knew something was off with the entire situation. I could tell by the plea in her eyes that she suspected I knew what it was. Her voice was near a whisper when she spoke.

90

"Why did you say, 'the castle is hardly empty?' What's going on, Jeffrey?"

I owed her an apology for so many things—for the night I'd kissed her, for the fear I knew she experienced now, and for my inability to bring myself to explain anything tonight. I hoped at least, as I reached to thumb a piece of earth from her brow, that she could feel the apology I didn't wish to give her in front of Jane, by the way I touched her.

"In the morning, I'm sure you'll understand everything but, for now, let's just all get some sleep, okay?"

Her face had softened when I touched her, but I watched her eyes harden toward me once again as I spoke. I knew to her it looked as if I once again refused to give her the explanation she deserved.

"In the morning. Right. Have a good night. Thanks for the bed."

She turned away, and I took my place by the fire. Morning couldn't come soon enough.

Kathleen spent the night glued to the bed by the weight of Jane's left leg and arm draped heavily against her, her mind churning over the events of the past day, confusion making her sick with worry.

91

None of it made sense—not the innkeepers' strange behavior or the attack they'd experienced—not the sudden appearance of Jeffrey or his unusual home. Even the mattress she lay on made her nervous. Curiosity had caused her to reach her hand over the side of the bed to feel the material, and it truly felt as if the entire thing had been sewn by hand. She was almost certain if she were to pull back the blanket she'd find no manufacturer label. Who and where did people make their own mattresses anymore?

Eventually, the whirlwind of thoughts exhausted her and she drifted into an uncomfortable and restless sleep, only to be awakened the next morning by the sound of Jeffrey's front door swinging open as the deep voice of a Scot filled the room.

"Jeffrey, I apologize for waking ye, but Grace says she needs to see ye right away, that ye are to be making a travel forward today. She wants to speak with ye…"

The man's voice trailed off as Kathleen threw Jane's arm off her waist so that she could sit up in the bed, causing the man's eyes to lock on her for the first time.

"Ach, I apologize lass, I dinna know that Jeffrey…" the man allowed his speech to drift as he scooted back uncomfortably.

Just as the stranger started to leave, Kathleen saw Jeffrey leap up from his place beside the fire.

"Eoghanan, wait. This isn't what it looks like at all."

92

Kathleen stood, leaning to poke a hard finger into Jane's ribs to wake her. "Get up." She muttered in Jane's direction as the man spoke once more.

"There are two of them, Jeffrey? Was one no enough for ye?"

Kathleen didn't like the stranger's insinuation and took a step forward to squelch his assumption. "Excuse me? Who are you to make such an accusation?"

His eyes grew wide as she spoke, the expression on his face changing from one of silent condemnation to utter shock as he turned his attention back to Jeffrey. "She's American?"

Jeffrey nodded, and Kathleen's brows pulled together as she waited for Jeffrey's response.

"Yes. Let's go get Grace."

The intruder left without question, and Kathleen immediately moved to block Jeffrey from following. "Nu-uh, explain. Now! Why did he ask that? Of course I'm American. Hasn't he ever seen an American before? And why…" Kathleen stopped as she looked Jeffrey over, a tan linen shirt covering his upper body, his lower half covered by a similar, unfamiliar material. She'd noticed in the dark, but in the daylight he looked even more ridiculous, like he should have been in some sort of period play. "Why are you dressed that way? Why do I feel like I've fallen down the rabbit hole?"

His answer sent a wave of panic and fear rushing through her.

"Because Kathleen, you kind of have."

Chapter 16

One thing Kathleen learned from their move to Scotland was that in times of crisis, she clearly had her shit far more together than Jane. While usually very collected, Jane's reaction to traumatic or frightening events was not a healthy one. If Kathleen believed Jane's reaction to their supposed attack was ridiculous, it was only because she'd not yet seen her go into a state of full-on denial over the next shock that would come their way.

After Grace's husband, Eoghanan, returned to Jeffrey's cabin with Grace in tow, they'd been forced to listen to a story so elaborate and unbelievable in its possibility that Kathleen would have been worried if Jane had accepted such news at face value. But after spending the entire day at McMillan Castle, surrounded by people dressed in clothes clearly made by hand and facilities entirely without modern conveniences, she found herself with little choice but to believe what they'd been told—

that instead of being attacked, the rocks they'd thrown had sent them tumbling into the seventeenth century.

While Jane had spent the afternoon glued to Grace's side, babbling and growing rather hysterical in her insistence that all of this was some huge elaborate ruse, Kathleen had spent the majority of the day observing and reflecting on this impossible truth.

Truthfully, it explained many things Kathleen knew Jane had wondered about for months. No wonder Jane had been unable to track down a cell number for Grace or that she'd had such difficulty locating an address.

Kathleen knew if she'd been alone, everything wouldn't have been so easy for her to accept. Rather than worrying over how to make her friend see the truth, she would have been seriously concerned over her own sanity. But with Jane experiencing the same thing, combined with Grace's absence for months, it was the only thing that really made any sense, even as impossible as it all seemed.

She couldn't begin to wrap her mind around how a thing such as time travel could exist, but Kathleen figured that many of life's biggest truths were that way anyway. Best not to overwhelm oneself with trying to figure it out when all that really mattered was that it undoubtedly existed.

The revelation of time travel didn't only shine light on all of Jane's questions about her sister, but it also gave Kathleen pause over Jeffrey's behavior so many nights before.

It wasn't that Kathleen believed a man's kiss to be a promise of a life spent together—she'd been around and dated enough men to know that, for many, a kiss could be given out as casually as one would offer a stick of gum to a stranger. That, or a kiss was simply deemed a necessary act one had to complete before moving on to explore what lay south of a woman's waistline. But Jeffrey's kiss had been none of those things. Although it held no promise, he'd not given it casually.

Instead, it held a sense of knowing so strong that it had taken Kathleen's breath away, and she knew it had Jeffrey's as well. He'd kissed her when she'd been angry and confused as to his behavior, and the moment his lips touched hers, she'd understood—he didn't want to fall for her, but his kiss was an undeniable admission that he had.

She didn't know him, not really, but for years she'd listened to Jane's stories and, little by little, year by year, she'd fallen for the idea of Jeffrey Oakes. And to Kathleen, the idea was enough, for there he could remain at a perfectly safe distance, unable to hurt her, incapable of shaking up the plans she'd worked so hard to lay out for her life.

His kiss had shaken up everything. In that moment she'd realized that her gut had always been right—if she met him, she would fall for him. And fall for him, she had, the first moment she'd looked up to see the spaghetti stain splattered across his shirt. His kiss had been affirmation that he cared for her as well.

Why then had he left so suddenly, making no effort to explain his behavior in the days or weeks that followed? These were the questions Kathleen had wrestled with every day since the kiss and only now, as she watched the sun fall over her first day in the seventeenth century, did she wonder if she knew the answers to the questions that ate at her.

Jeffrey knew that when he and Cooper left they were coming back here. Had he left her to protect them both—believing that such feelings were pointless if they could never exist in the same century? Maybe, maybe not, but she knew this much—she'd been a coward the day Jeffrey had come by Jane's apartment to say goodbye. She wouldn't allow herself to be so cowardly again.

Most people around McMillan Castle didn't bother knocking, least of all my young son, his mother, or Eoghanan, so it surprised me to hear the sound of knuckles against my door just after sunset.

"Come in," I shouted toward the doorway, not thinking for a moment that I would turn to find Kathleen stepping inside. After the way I'd treated her at every one of our meetings, I'd been sure she would stay as far away from me as possible.

I smiled as I stood to move toward her, hoping once again that she would see the apology I'd yet to give her. "It's too dark for you to walk all the way from the castle over here by yourself."

She shook her head, stepping fully inside so that she could close the door behind her. Immediately, the space between us seemed to turn electric, that same tension building that had existed the last time we'd found ourselves alone together.

"No, the sun was still up when I left. It wasn't that dark."

"How's Jane?" From what I'd seen, Kathleen seemed to be adjusting to the shock of learning a witch had spelled her into the past rather impressively. Jane, on the other hand, was freaking out enough for the both of them.

"Um..." she shifted from foot to foot and smiled not at me but at the wall behind me. I could tell that she avoided my gaze intentionally. "Well, you remember that day Jane faked the headache?"

I nodded, lust surging through every inch of me at the memory. Of course, I remembered. It hadn't left my mind for a moment.

"Yeah, I don't think she'll be having to fake a headache tomorrow. Our heads were already throbbing but she's downed enough, I'm not even sure what it is, to render a horse unconscious. Last I saw her, Eoghanan was hauling her off to our bedroom."

"And how are you handling everything?" I wanted to reach out and touch her, to try and comfort her in some way, but I refrained.

"I'm fine. I mean, I may just still be in shock. It's very possible I could come totally unglued tomorrow but most likely not to the extent that Jane has."

"No," I shook my head. I'd yet to hear of anyone quite as rattled by the experience as Jane seemed to be. "Most likely not."

I stepped back to make way for her movement as she paced uncomfortably around the small space of my living room. "Is everything okay? You know, I'm glad you stopped by, I've been meaning to…"

She interrupted me, spinning to point a finger in my direction. "I'm changing the subject, okay?"

When I said nothing, she continued.

"You were trying to prevent feelings from developing, right? Because there was no point."

Of course that's why I'd left her after the kiss. What sort of a fool would have done so otherwise? She was worked up—her breathing escalated and her face flushed with nervousness. I wanted to pull her into my arms and keep her there all night. Instead, I nodded.

"Okay. Okay, that's good then. Umm…" shyly she stepped toward me, her voice shaky as she spoke. "I'm going to kiss you now."

I smiled as we met each other in the center of the room, pulling her hard against me as I reached her. And this time, I didn't pull away from our kiss until the need for air required it.

Chapter 17

Kathleen sat gazing into the fire, a blanket draped around the both of them as Jeffrey wrapped his arms around her, resting his head on her shoulder.

"Will you return home?"

Kathleen felt the tension in Jeffrey's chest as he asked her the question. They'd not even been there a day, and it honestly wasn't something Kathleen had thought on very much at all. She knew why Jeffrey asked it. It had been fear of distance that had caused him to retreat from her before. It only made sense that after their evening spent kissing and talking by the fire that this would be on his mind once again.

"I don't know." It was the honest answer, but something within her grew heavy as she said it.

Jeffrey kissed her lightly on the cheek, rubbing the sides of her arms in a gesture that Kathleen felt was more of his way of shaking the tension from himself than warming her arms.

101

"Of course you don't know. Why would you yet? What do you think Jane will do?"

That was a far easier question. Even though Jane was still far too frightened to have put any thought into it, Kathleen knew well enough what Jane would decide to do. She, of course, would stay.

Sure, the allure of adventure had helped in Jane's decision to join her in Scotland and to put up her trust fund for the restoration of the castle, but Kathleen knew the real driving force behind her decision had been her desire to get closer to Grace and Cooper. They were the most important people in her life. If they were here, Jane would adjust to making her life here as well.

"She'll stay. As much as she'll miss *General Hospital* and her coffee maker, she wouldn't want to miss watching Cooper grow up."

Jeffrey smiled into her ear, and she knew what he thought even before he said it. "Well, I'm glad. Even as crazy as she is, I don't want Cooper to grow up without her either. But you know what she'll really miss?"

Kathleen nodded, Jeffrey's nose brushing the side of her cheek as she moved her head up and down, the sensation a delicious one. "Her car."

"Yes. She'll be mourning that baby for months."

"Longer, I expect."

Jeffrey reached around her, tucking the end of the blanket around their feet. "Yes, you're probably right. What about you? If you did stay, what would you be leaving behind?"

Kathleen leaned her head back against him as she thought.

"It shouldn't be so difficult for me to think of things, but truthfully, very little. I have no family, and Jane's really my only very close friend. Still," Kathleen paused, thinking on her beloved castle, the dream she'd spent so long preparing for. "I don't know if I could bring myself to leave Cagair Castle, to allow it to return to such a state of disrepair."

Jeffrey sighed behind her, standing suddenly, leaving her back cold as he extended a hand. "It's time to take you back to the castle. Otherwise, you'll be the subject of unfair gossip come morning. I have an idea, though, if you'd like to hear it."

Kathleen took his hands and was quickly pulled against his chest as he wrapped his arms around her.

"I'll be honest with you, Kathleen, and this sort of soul-bearing is something that does not come easily to me."

He pulled away just enough so that he could cup her face with his hands, locking his eyes on her with such intensity it made Kathleen's heart pump almost painfully with the emotion she felt in his gaze.

"I want you to decide to stay here. I know I don't know you well, but I'd like to, and I can't do that if you're living hundreds of years from now. I don't have the luxury of a choice. I won't leave my son here."

He paused and Kathleen could see that he struggled for the words he meant to say. Smiling for a brief moment, he leaned forward to kiss her forehead, still keeping his grip on her face.

"Give me a few days to help you make your decision."

"To help me?" Kathleen smiled, her cheeks, smashed together by the pressure of his hands.

He kissed her softly, leaving her breathless and weak.

"To make you fall in love with me, Kathleen. If in three days you love me more than you love that old castle, then stay. If you decide to return to the present, then you have that much more research and experience to put into the renovation."

It frightened Kathleen half to death to think that she was already halfway in love with him, but she couldn't say that. She wouldn't confess something so crazy.

"Why three days?"

"Because that's how long it will take us to travel to your castle."

Excitement rose in Kathleen at the thought of being able to see her beloved castle in its prime—filled with the very people that supposedly haunted it in the present. She couldn't think of anything she'd rather do, but she still didn't understand why Jeffrey suggested it.

"Why do you want to take me to my castle?"

He released her face, stepping back a pace to hold up a finger.

"Well, for one, it might help Jane accept everything. She's used to seeing your castle in its disintegrated state. If she saw it now, whole and perfect—well, I don't know how she could deny that any of this is real after that."

It was an excellent point. Kathleen smiled, thinking of what was bound to be Jane's over-the-top reaction.

"And point two?"

He winked at her and lifted his second finger. "Travel is an excellent way to get to know someone. It will give me several uninterrupted days to show you how charming I can be."

Kathleen laughed and bent to fold the blanket they'd been sitting under.

"Anything else?"

"Well, yes, actually. Do you know how to ride a horse?"

Kathleen frowned, the prospect of spending days on the back of a horse, truly unappealing. "No. Can't say that I do."

Her answer thrilled Jeffrey. "Perfect. If you can't ride, you'll be forced to sit right in front of me for the entire journey. And if three days of that doesn't make you fall in love with me...well, I don't know what will."

Finally, Dad was letting him in on the good stuff. He'd not even been mad at him when he told Mom about Aunt Jane being in Scotland. Now Dad was even asking him for advice.

"You don't think it's entirely selfish of me, Coop? To ask her to stay here? That's sure a lot to ask of somebody who hardly knows me."

Cooper shook his head, helping his dad roll up his blanket as they packed for his trip. Why did grown-ups always think that love needed to take such a long time? Sometimes, you just know. Hadn't he already been through this with Mom and E-o?

"No, Dad. It's not selfish if she loves you too and she wants to stay. Asking her isn't making her do anything. Besides, you know if later she wanted to leave, Morna would always help her."

Dad tied a rope around the blanket, tossing it into the pile of all the other items he still needed to pack on his horse. "You're right, but son, I talked some big talk with her the other night and now I'm second-guessing myself just a little."

"Dad, she likes you. Didn't you say she came over to your cabin and kissed you! Girls don't come over to your cabin and do that. She has to like you already."

"Maybe you're right. Still, I just don't know if three days is enough time."

Cooper could see Kathleen, Aunt Jane, and E-o heading in their direction and knew he only had a few more moments to give his dad a pep talk. He moved and pulled on his dad's hand so he would crouch down in front of him. Once their faces were at equal level, Cooper reached up and placed his hands on either side of his dad's face.

"Okay, they're coming, so you listen up. Three days is the perfect amount of time. Just think about all those fairy tales that you and Bebop read to me—all the magic happens in three days. Now, don't you disappoint me, Dad. I'll stay here and watch after Mom, but I expect you to come back here with a wife."

Chapter 18

Day 1—On The Road

I owed Eoghanan a great deal for accompanying us—there was absolutely no doubt about that. Not only did he provide the navigational skills that I lacked, but he'd also been placed in charge of riding with Jane. God bless the man.

Even without a hangover, I imagined Jane would have been uncomfortable on a horse. But now, with her head hurting so badly her eyes looked like they might bleed, Eoghanan was forced to listen to her moaning at the horse's every step.

"Jane, can ye no see that yer wailing is only making it worse? Just lean back and breathe through yer nose as ye look at the sky."

Jane sniffled but did lean back against her brother-in-law's shoulder as instructed.

"Fine, but I swear to you guys, if we get there and all of this is revealed to be some sort of elaborate made-for-TV prank. If that castle isn't one hundred percent restored and perfect, I am going to kick every single one of your asses."

Kathleen laughed as she spoke, and the vibration against my chest shot straight down to my groin. I shifted back on the horse so she wouldn't be able to tell what she did to me.

"Jane, you did this all to yourself, sweetheart. What did you think was going to happen as you chugged down cup after cup?"

"Shut up, Kathleen."

I nudged Kathleen playfully in the ribs, whispering in her ear so that Jane wouldn't hear.

"She's a mean drunk, isn't she?"

She laughed and leaned into me, the scent of her hair causing my stomach to tighten. She didn't ever mean to, but she had no idea the effect her every movement, every word, had on me.

"I wouldn't know. I know last night isn't any indication, but she's really not much of a drinker. Even in college, it just wasn't her thing."

I nodded, reaching up with my left hand to brush a strand of hair from her face.

"Cooper and I have a theory."

"Oh," she laughed that deep, sexy laugh that made me want to pull her off of this horse and roll around in the grass with her for hours. "What's that?"

"We think you must be an amazing singer."

Her head whipped around so that she could look at me straight on. "Why would you think that? I cannot even begin to tell you how terrible I am."

I shrugged, disbelieving her statement. There was no way a voice like that could not sing. "You have such a pleasant talking voice. We just figured that would translate over."

"Really? I always hated my voice. I used to pray, I mean, actually pray that one day someone would invent something that could change the pitch of your voice."

I rubbed her thigh with my thumb, noticing the small catch of her breath as I did so.

"That would be such a shame. Really, everything you say is sexy as hell."

She remained turned and her cheeks flushed pink at my words.

"Well, thank you, I guess. When I was growing up, I sure never would have thought someone would think that. I think I sound like a man."

"Not at all." I leaned forward to brush her nose with my own. "Now sing something so I can see if you're telling the truth. I don't believe you at all."

She chuckled, spinning to face the front. "Ha. Only if you do it first."

"Sure, why not?" With that, I belted out a few lines of a song my dad had sung to me as a child about an old boat that sunk over the Great Lakes during a storm. I kept going until Eoghanan stopped me.

"For God's sake, Jeffrey, ye are making the birds weep. I beg ye to stop, man."

I laughed and nudged Kathleen so she would know it was her turn. "See? There's no way you can be worse than that."

"Oh, yes there is."

To my astounding surprise, she hadn't lied. She was way worse than me and, for some reason, the sound of her screechy, off-pitch voice belting out *I Wanna Dance With Somebody* made her all the more endearing.

K athleen leaned half of her body against the trunk of the tree, pushing her butt outward to stretch her shockingly sore muscles. It astounded her how exhausting riding was. Her body hurt so badly she couldn't sleep.

She seemed to be the only one with that problem. They'd ridden until sundown and then set up camp a short distance from a stream. Each of them stretched around the fire—Eoghanan and Jeffrey each in their own makeshift sleeping bag and Jane and Kathleen in the same one to keep warm. Despite the cool breeze, the clingy cuddler that Jane always became after falling asleep had made Kathleen seek cooler air within the woods.

It was a beautiful night and every star appeared extraordinarily bright amongst the uncluttered sky. Gazing up at it, she kneaded her fingers into the muscles of her rear end, doing her best to work out the soreness from the strange angle.

A familiar voice from behind caused her to jump before relaxing into Jeffrey's arms as he wrapped them around her.

"Do you need some help with that? I'd be happy to work that soreness out for you."

She poked him in the ribs before facing him, turning her head up to kiss him gently on the mouth.

"I'm sure you would but that would be moving just a little too quickly."

Jeffrey pulled her in close, speaking softly into her ear. "I didn't mean that as a come on, Kathleen. Not to say that I don't want to make love to you. I do, very much so."

He leaned against her for emphasis, and Kathleen swallowed the hard knot of anticipation that rose up in her throat.

"But even if you wished it, even if you were ready, I wouldn't do it here—not in the middle of the woods with Eoghanan and Jane just a few feet away. You deserve much better than that. I meant it as a genuine question. Riding is brutal on an ass that isn't used to it. You'd feel much better if you let someone work out the tension."

Kathleen stepped away to get a better look at him to try and gauge his sincerity. "No funny business?"

Winking, he reached for her, slowly leading her to his pallet. "I promise."

"Okay…" hesitantly she lowered herself to her knees, gently laying down on her stomach over his blankets. "I could go for a massage."

His hands were strong. They felt wonderful against the balled-up segments of muscle. Kathleen sighed as the tension slowly left her.

"I know what you're doing, you know."

She could hear the smile in his voice as he leaned in closer to whisper.

"Do you now? What's that?"

"You're being kind and caring and very well-behaved, in the hopes that I'll fall in love with you."

He pinched her bottom, making her jump. "I'm not always so well-behaved, but I try to always be kind and caring." He hesitated a moment before leaning down so that his every breath sent tingles down her spine as he spoke. "Is any of it working?"

Her voice was breathless as she answered, "yes, I'm afraid it is."

Chapter 19

Day Two—On The Road

The second and final night of our journey before reaching the castle, Eoghanan treated us all with a stay inside a small village inn, having had enough experience with twenty-first century women to understand their dislike for sleeping under the stars.

The inn had exactly three rooms. Eoghanan rented them all, saying he would feel much better about leaving the women in a room by themselves if he knew no other guests would be admitted for the evening. It also meant that Eoghanan and I would each have a room of our own and, though he didn't say it, I suspected that played some part in his decision to rent the entire place out.

Not that I'd be getting any sleep regardless. My mind was much too filled with all things Kathleen. So far, everything was wonderful, but I still couldn't be sure as to her feelings. She'd admitted nothing, given nothing away as to what she was thinking.

Surely, there was no way she would go back. How could she? Not when I knew she felt the same way I did. I mean, I was ninety-nine percent sure she felt the same; although, the only brief hint I'd received to make me think that way was her admission that my efforts were working.

Still, there was a difference in learning to like someone, in wanting to spend more time in their company, and being crazy enough about them to remain in a time so different from your own. It was a lot to ask her, and it was a decision she would have to reach entirely on her own.

I reached my hand down into the sack of my belongings sitting next to the bed I now lay in, fumbling for the small box my father had given me just before I left—my mother's ring. I wouldn't pull it out until after she'd told me her decision, until I knew for sure one way or the other where Kathleen's heart lay.

Why could there never just be two beds? Why did she always get stuck with Jane? Her cuddling was one thing but, on this night, Kathleen was also treated to a symphony of snores coming from her close friend. Even if her mind hadn't been busy turning over a million different thoughts, she wouldn't have been able to sleep a wink.

Sliding off the side of the bed to free herself, Kathleen stood and paced the room. Obviously, she wasn't leaving. She couldn't. The castle was special to her, but it wouldn't keep her warm at night. It wouldn't give her the family she always wanted. It was only a building. In time, someone else would come along and finish the job she'd started.

Her mind turned back to Jeffrey; she could feel his presence on the other side of the wall, could picture him spread out over the bed, his eyes closed in a gentle slumber. She wanted to be right beside him, wanted to wake him by pressing her body against his so that he could work out all of the tension from her body like he'd promised. Only this time, she didn't wish for him to do so in the form of a massage.

Sure, she'd acted as if she wasn't ready for such intimacy the night before, but not because she didn't want him, because she wanted him so badly it scared her.

Kathleen snorted, thinking back on Jeffrey and his belief that he needed three days to make her fall for him—he'd truly needed none.

Crazy as it might seem, she knew where this would lead. She could see their future together, and every bit of it seemed inevitable. What sense was there in delaying it? She knew what she wanted.

Moving to the door, she pulled it open as quietly as she could. Finding the hallway empty, she ran on the tips of her toes the short distance to Jeffrey's room. Just as she reached for the handle, she heard movement on the stairwell. The sound of approaching steps startled her. In her rush not to be caught in the hallway, she flung the door to Jeffrey's room open, slamming it loudly behind her as she stepped inside.

"Kathleen?" The room was dark, but she could hear him sit up in the bed. The alertness in his voice told her he'd not been sleeping either. "What are you doing here?"

Leaning against the doorway, she worked to catch her breath, hoping the commotion hadn't awakened the whole house.

"Well, besides embarrassing myself, I…" Kathleen took a step toward him as he climbed out of bed to approach her. All he wore was a pair of linen pants, his bare chest outlined only by the moon's light that shined a soft glow through the window. "I…wanted to tell you something."

Jeffrey's hands found hers in the darkness and he bent to kiss her, pressing her back against the doorway, the darkness immediately increasing the intimacy of his touch. It seemed to make him bolder than usual, and Kathleen reveled in it, gasping as his teeth moved to graze her earlobe and his hands moved to her breast.

"Jeffrey," his name came out shaky. Her lips trembled as Jeffrey pulled them deep into his mouth.

"What is it?" Jeffrey's breath was warm and rapid against her chest and his hand moved to Kathleen's cheek, where he gently thumbed her brow as he spoke. "What did you want to tell me?"

Kathleen couldn't remember anything she'd meant to say, her entire body flooded with such indescribable desire, she could think of nothing else.

"I...I wanted to say that, I'd like to stay here tonight...with you."

The noise that came from Jeffrey as he pushed her hard against the wall came from deep within his throat, a noise of hunger and desire that made Kathleen's entire body quiver with anticipation.

He said nothing, only turned her around so that he could undo her laces, quickly sending her dress to the floor. Kathleen gasped at the sensation of air rushing over her exposed body, moaning as Jeffrey palmed her naked breasts, pressing her back against his front as he slid one hand down to cup the center between her legs.

"Are you sure? We don't have..."

She loved that despite being in the thralls of his desire, he still worried for her, that he still didn't want to press her into something she wasn't ready for. He worried needlessly—she was far more than ready. Reaching her arm around her back, she slipped her hand in between their bodies, dipping her hand into the waistline of Jeffrey's pants in answer to his question.

He pulled her hand away, grabbing onto both of her arms as he turned her toward him before removing his bottoms. Taking her hand, he led her to the bed, pressing her back against it as he slowly crawled on top of her.

He moved slowly, trailing kisses from her toes to her naval, stopping to suckle at her breasts until she moaned and moved against him, her legs spreading themselves naturally, encouraging him to begin his entry.

He needed no further encouragement. Kathleen smiled against his mouth as he leaned upward to kiss her, sliding himself inside as they moved together.

The moon beat down through the window, shining a soft, white light upon their lovemaking.

Kathleen lost herself in the moment. Her confession of love and her decision to stay could wait until morning.

Chapter 20

Day Three—Cagair Castle

The castle was even more amazing than she'd imagined it and, to her pleasant surprise, the changes she and Jane had begun to make on its restoration seemed to be headed in the right direction. At least she could be satisfied knowing that had she continued her work on the structure, she'd have been restoring it correctly.

They'd arrived to find the castle's main residents away—something that Eoghanan informed them was no real surprise. Apparently, Lennox MacChristy and his sons spent a good deal of time traveling and had only acquired the castle recently. After the death of the castle's former laird, the people requested that Lennox MacChristy take his place.

Still, MacChristy's men had opened the castle to them at Eoghanan's request, and it was a sheer thrill for Kathleen to be able to explore every inch.

And, just as Jeffrey had hoped, it had done the trick in bringing some finality to Jane's question over the authenticity of their travel through time. She could argue the truth no longer.

Kathleen took Jeffrey's hand as they walked around the castle's tallest tower that looked out onto the sea.

It was her favorite room in the entire castle, with its surrounding windows opening the room up to light that seemed rare in such old structures. It was the one room that even in present day seemed to withstand the decay of time.

Moving toward one of the windows, Kathleen turned to Jeffrey, ready to tell him all that she'd meant to the night before.

"It's been three days, you know?"

Jeffrey leaned into her, pressing his forehead gently against her own.

"And?"

Kathleen kissed him, her heart smiling as she did so. Who would have thought her grandmother's inheritance would have sent her on such an incredible journey and, in the end, gifted her with something so precious?

"You didn't need three days. I've loved you since the first."

McMillan Castle—Three Days Later

She cried as I asked her for her hand that day up in the castle tower, and I'm man enough to admit that as I slipped my mother's ring onto Kathleen's finger that I shed a tear or two of my own.

Now, as we rode back up to our new home, I smiled at the sight of the rest of our family awaiting our arrival. I'd not kept my word with Cooper—I wasn't arriving home with a new wife, but when Cooper learned why, I didn't think that he'd mind all that much.

I wanted to marry Kathleen in front of my son, my father, Grace—all of the people that had wished such happiness for me for so long. I nudged our horse to pick up its speed. I couldn't wait to get home.

We would be married by nightfall, and then our real journey together would begin.

Jane, on the other hand, would now have to find someone else besides my future wife to cuddle up to at night.

Turn the page for a Sneak Peek of the next book in the series, ***Love Beyond Compare.***

Sneak Peek of Love Beyond Compare (Book 5)

CHAPTER 1

McMillan Castle, Scotland—December 28, 1648

Tiny, freezing toes pressed themselves against the side of my leg, jolting me from a dream that would have made even a nun's blood race.

"It's always the good ones, isn't it, Coop? You can never wake me while I'm dreaming about spiders, or worms, or sharks."

"Huh?"

"Never mind." I squirmed away instinctively, rolling as I used my hands to push the way-too-early-rising six year old to the other side of the bed. Instantly, Cooper's sleepy voice pleaded with me as his heat-seeking toes sought the warmth of my side once again.

"Ohhh, please don't, Aunt Jane. I'm freezing."

I kept my eyelids closed, doing my best to hold on to any remaining fragment of my dream.

"Coop, I love you but you know the rule—you aren't supposed to wake anybody up before six a.m."

"First of all, you know that's not the rule anymore, Aunt Jane. We don't have those electric clocks here, so I have to wait until the sun rises. And second of all…"

He paused for dramatic effect, and I could all but see his little fingers ticking away his points. After a long pause, he continued.

"I didn't come to wake you up. I came to sleep. I'm soooo tired."

I heard him yawn in the darkness, and I knew then what had sent him fleeing from his own room in the middle of the night. "Baby Violet keeping you up?"

"Yep. She sure does cry a lot. I can hear her through the walls. I know that she's supposed to get more fun later, but right now…I just wish she'd stayed inside Mom."

I laughed and allowed my eyes to open as I rolled to face him, his outline illuminated by the moonlight streaming in through the window. I could just make out the smattering of freckles across his face, his dirty blond curls shining in the moonlight. "I'm pretty sure that your mother felt the very same way about me for a long time."

"No way. I bet you were always fun."

Cooper was the only person on Earth who thought so highly of me.

"Believe me, I wasn't. Now," my mouth pulled open, catching the remnants of Cooper's yawn, "you ready to get some shut eye?"

124

Cooper made his teeth chatter for effect. "Not until my toes are warm."

Reluctantly, I pushed myself upright in the bed. "Okay, fine. Stick your toes up here."

He shifted himself in the bed, spinning so that his head was near the bed's end as he thrust his feet toward my face. "Thank you. I'm pretty sure they were about to fall right off."

"Oh yes, I'm sure they were." I laughed as I rubbed my hands back and forth over his feet. "Why don't you wear socks to bed? I know that you have some."

"You see, I always start out in socks. Mom always makes me put them on but, somehow, I toss and I turn and they end up disappearing. I have a theory. I don't think they actually disappear, of course. I think the little fairies that Bebop says live in the Highlands come to live inside the walls during colder months, and they take my socks at night to use as sleeping bags to keep warm. Works good for them, but it sure makes my feet cold."

"Wow, that's...that's quite the theory, Coop." Cooper was ridiculously intelligent for his age—always had been.

"I know it is."

His feet were now warm to the touch, and I gave them a pat so he'd know I was finished as I helped him spin so that his head was back at the top of the bed.

"You ready for bed now? I promise not to cry and wake you like baby Vi."

"Are you sure? You've been just about as whiny as her lately, Aunt Jane."

The things that came out of that little man's mouth never ceased to amaze me. "What?"

He moved in close for a snuggle, no doubt an attempt to soften the blow. I allowed him to rest his head on my shoulder as he spoke again.

"You heard me. Do you not like it here, Aunt Jane? 'Cause I would miss you like crazy, but I don't want you to stay here just for me."

"Oh, Coop." My heart squeezed suddenly, causing an ache to root itself deep inside my chest. I couldn't imagine what it would be like to have a child of my own—the constant overwhelming love so strong it was almost painful, and the way their words could devastate you completely. "I'm not staying here just for you. Everyone that I care most about in the world is here. I'm not going anywhere. I don't want to."

"Oh, good. That's really good, Aunt Jane."

He yawned and I knew now that his fear was comforted, it wouldn't be long before he drifted off to sleep. Not that he would stay asleep for very long. Cooper had a reputation for rousing hours before anyone else of Mitchell descent ever dreamed of waking.

I leaned over to kiss the top of his head and hunkered back down in the bed. Cooper's observational skills were as keen as ever. I wasn't unhappy, only dissatisfied with the lack of purpose in my life here. With each passing day, I felt as if I were one step closer to the cliff's edge, to losing my mind and, with it, everything that made me, me.

I had nothing to do with all of my time here. And time seemed to last forever in the seventeenth century. I now believed that anyone in present day who ever said they wished they could escape to a different time to enjoy a slower pace of life obviously never thought about what exactly that meant.

For me, the unmarried sister of the laird's sister-in-law, it meant I lived my life in a weird state of pointlessness. I contributed nothing to the people who provided me with a lifestyle of pure luxury compared to most of those living on the outskirts of the castle—people who worked for everything they had, rising with the sun and working well into the night, all the while remaining thankful for each and every blessing.

My lack of real responsibility around the castle, or keep, made me feel like a lazy, spoiled moocher. And slowly, if it continued this way, I knew it would drive me mad in a matter of months.

Not to say I lived my life with a whole lot of purpose in present-day time. I knew what my family's wealth had afforded me. At times, when I was younger, I took full advantage, wasting years doing just exactly what I pleased rather than participating as a productive, responsible member of society.

Fun and carefree I might have appeared, but that lifestyle slowly ate away at me in my old life just like it was doing here.

127

Difference was, there were so many more distractions in the twenty-first century, so many more mind-numbing forms of entertainment and social activities to fill my days with and keep myself from thinking on it all that much. Here, the only thing I had to do with my time was think.

And think, I had. What Cooper didn't know was that my strange, whiny behavior the past few weeks wasn't out of unhappiness but instead out of anticipation and anxiety. I knew what I wanted, what I needed to do with all of my spare time, but I knew that it wouldn't be considered appropriate. If I asked permission, which I absolutely refused to do anyway, no matter the time period, it would be denied.

I would have to keep my plans a secret from all but a few.

I woke the next morning to the shock of finding Cooper still sleeping soundly next to me. Baby Violet had certainly changed the flow of everything around the castle, but for none more so than Cooper, if she had the power to wear him out enough that he slept past five a.m.

I slipped out of the bed as silently as I could manage, moving across the room to wash my face in the basin of freezing water. With weather as cold as it was now, I wasn't sure it was worth cleaning my face. For the sake of vanity, I gritted my teeth while I scrubbed the sleep from my eyes before pulling up my hair and dressing in a simple but thick green gown suitable for keeping out the bitter cold while riding. Not nearly as suitable as a pair of jeans and some boots, but it was as good as I could get away with here.

Once dressed, I stepped out into the hallway and right into the pathway of my sleep-deprived sister.

"Did Coop crash with you?"

Dark circles hung on the bottom of her eyes and I moved in to give her a hug. "Yes, he did. You look like crap, Grace."

She groaned into my ear, allowing herself to relax against me. I had to lock my legs to keep us both up.

"Of course I look like crap. I think Violet is part bat. She's more nocturnal than even Cooper. I was hoping that she'd start sleeping at night more after the first few months, but she's nine months old now and she's still so fussy at night."

I glanced down at the small swell of Grace's belly. "Well, hopefully this third baby will give you an easier time."

Grace pulled away. I could tell she was about to cry. Exhaustion always did that to her, and understandably so. I knew she was excited for the next baby, due the end of May, but juggling a six year old, a nine month old, and being four months pregnant were a lot, especially when she refused to use the castle help that Eoghanan and the castle laird, Baodan, continually offered her. She'd raised Cooper with only Jeffrey's help for years, and she was determined to raise her other children the same way.

"I sure hope so. Kathleen has Violet right now. I think I'm going to try and rest awhile."

"That's exactly what you should do, but before you go, do you know where Eoghanan is? I need to talk to him about something."

"Uh…" She hesitated and I wondered if she was about to fall asleep where she stood. "I think he said something about rescuing Violet from Kathleen's singing, so he may have the baby now. I'm really not sure."

"Okay." I patted her on the shoulder and turned her back in the direction she'd been headed. "Get some rest, Grace. I'll find him."

To read the rest of *Love Beyond Compare*, get your copy now.

About the Author

Bethany Claire is the author of the Scottish, time travel romance novels Love Beyond Time, Love Beyond Reason, A Conall Christmas—Novella, Love Beyond Hope, Love Beyond Measure, In Due Time—A Novella, and other series titles coming soon. She grew up in the Texas Panhandle.

Connect with me online:

http://www.bethanyclaire.com
http://twitter.com/BClaireAuthor
http://facebook.com/bethanyclaire
http://www.pinterest.com/bclaireauthor

If you enjoyed reading *In Due Time – A Novella,* I would appreciate it if you would help others enjoy this book, too.

Recommend it. Help other readers find this book by recommending it to friends, readers' groups and discussion boards.

Review it. Please tell other readers why you like this book by reviewing it at the retailer of your choice. If you do write a review, please send me an email to bclaire@bethanyclaire.com so I can thank you with a personal email, or you can visit my website at http://www.bethanyclaire.com

Join the Bethany Claire Newsletter!

Sign up for my newsletter to receive up-to-date information of books, new releases, events, and promotions.

http://bethanyclaire.com/contact.php - mailing-list

Acknowledgments

No book is a one-person project. While the stories are my own, no book could ever reach completion without the countless hours of help invested by so many others. Your work allows me to do what I love and for that, I thank you.

Mom, thank you for all that you do. I know this one really tested us both. Thanks for your patience and for not giving up on me even though I seem to have a really bad habit of testing the limits of my self-inflicted deadlines.

As always, thank you DeWanna, for your wonderful suggestions and friendship.

Lastly, to my proofreading team members: Karen Corboy, Elizabeth Halliday, and Marsha Orien—having your eyes on the manuscript helps more than you know. Thanks for your continued support, wonderful suggestions, and interest in my work. I hope that you enjoyed the process—hectic as it was this time around.

Books by Bethany Claire

Morna's Legacy Series

Love Beyond Time
Love Beyond Reason
A Conall Christmas – A Christmas Novella
Love Beyond Hope
Love Beyond Measure
In Due Time – A Novella
Love Beyond Compare
Love Beyond Dreams

CPSIA information can be obtained
at www.ICGtesting.com
Printed in the USA
BVOW03s1919181017
498071BV00001B/123/P